HORRIBLE HISTORIES

HORRIBLE HISTORIES

ON THIS HORRIBLE DAY IN HISTORY

I'M NOT VERY GOOD WITH DATES

TERRY DEARY

ILLUSTRATED BY
MARTIN BROWN

■SCHOLASTIC

For Martha Gavin – for serving the cause of history for four horrible years. TD

This book wouldn't have happened without the tremendous talents of the designer and editor. Thank you. MB

Published in the UK by Scholastic, 2025
Scholastic, Bosworth Avenue, Warwick, CV34 6UQ
Scholastic Ireland, 89E Lagan Road, Dublin Industrial Estate, Glasnevin, Dublin, D11 HP5F

SCHOLASTIC, HORRIBLE HISTORIES and associated logos are trademarks and/or registered trademarks of Scholastic Inc.

Text © Terry Deary, 2025
Cover and inside illustrations © Martin Brown, 2025

Contains material previously published in *Dreadul Diary*, *Mad Miscellany* and *Deadly Days*.

The moral rights of Terry Deary and Martin Brown have been asserted by them.

ISBN 978 0702 34396 4

A CIP catalogue record for this book is available from the British Library.

All rights reserved.
This book is sold subject to the condition that it shall not, by way of trade or otherwise, be lent, hired out or otherwise circulated in any form of binding or cover other than that in which it is published. No part of this publication may be reproduced, stored in a retrieval system, or transmitted in any form or by any other means (electronic, mechanical, photocopying, recording or otherwise) or used to train any artificial intelligence technologies without prior written permission of Scholastic Limited. Subject to EU law Scholastic Limited expressly reserves this work from the text and data mining exception.

Printed and bound in Great Britain by Clays Ltd, Elcograf S.p.A.
Paper made from wood grown in sustainable forests and other controlled sources.

10 9 8 7 6 5 4 3 2 1

www.scholastic.co.uk

For safety or quality concerns:
UK: www.scholastic.co.uk/productinformation
EU: www.scholastic.ie/productinformation

CONTENTS

January **9**

February **21**

March **33**

April **45**

May **57**

June **69**

July **79**

August **95**

September **107**

October **117**

November **131**

December **141**

**A YEAR. 365 DAYS.
WHAT'S THE WORST THAT
COULD HAPPEN?**

CHARLES THE BOLD'S BODY FOUND AFTER THE BATTLE OF NANCY – 7 JANUARY 1471

JANUARY

1 January 1660

Samuel Pepys begins his famous diary today. Entries include dreadful diary gems like, 'Today I went to see Major General Harrison hanged, drawn and quartered. He was looking as cheerful as any man could do in that condition.' The major ends up in four cheerful bits plus his head.

What sort of crimes could you be hanged for in Britain? Here are six swinging crimes…

Date of law	Crime
1603	Bigamy (getting married when you already have a wife or husband)
1671	Lying in wait with a plan to smash someone's nose
1699	Stealing from a shop anything worth more than 5 shillings (about £25)
1723	Poaching, sheep-stealing
1782	Being in the company of travellers
1810	Horse-stealing, putting on a disguise, stealing

2 January 1911

Sidney Street, London. Three terrorists hide in a house. Next day they're surrounded by hundreds of police and soldiers. After a seven-hour gun battle the house catches fire. A government minister watches the fire and lets them burn to death. This ruthless minister is a young man called Winston Churchill who will lead Britain (ruthlessly) through the Second World War in thirty years' time.

3 January 1804

Hammersmith, London. Local people are terrified by tales of a monstrous white ghost. One woman has already died of fright. Law Officer Smith sees a white figure and shoots it – the figure drops dead. It isn't a ghost, it's a bricklayer in white shirt and trousers. Oooops. Brick-layers of Hammersmith will be careful to change out of their white clothes before walking home in future.

4 January 1642

London. King Charles I marches into Parliament with his soldiers to arrest some MPs who are demanding the arrest of his queen. The gallant MPs gallantly run away through the back door as Charles comes in the front.

5 January 1941

London. Amy Johnson is a British superstar of the air with record flights around the world. In the Second World War she delivers planes around the country. Today she delivers her last. It crashes into the Thames. But why is it 100 miles off course? Why do search ships see two parachutes descend when Amy is flying alone? Why is her body never recovered? It's a mystery.

6 January

Twelfth Night. (That's to say the twelfth night after Christmas Day.) Take down your decorations or bad luck will strike. Good luck keeping track watching Shakespeare's play, 'Twelfth Night', which traditionally had a boy actor playing a girl character who dresses up as a boy but is really a girl.

7 January 1471

France. The body of Charles the Bold, Duke of Burgundy, has been found. In his last battle, at Nancy two days ago, he was defeated for the third time in twelve months. (You'd think he'd have learned after the first or second time, wouldn't you?) A young knight finds what's left of Charles' body once the wolves have had a nibble.

8 January 1815

Battle of New Orleans, USA. 6,000 Americans defeat 8,000 British soldiers. Hundreds of British are killed and thousands injured, but just eight Americans die. The Americans celebrate this day. For some reason the Brits do not.

9 January 1683

Whitehall, London. Do you have a pus-filled swelling on your neck? It could mean you have scrofula. Never mind, today King Charles II is organising the cure – the touch of the king's hand. He touches 24,000 sufferers in the first four years of his reign. Hope he washed his hands afterwards. Yeuch.

10 January 1863

London. Prime Minister Gladstone opens a fantastic new transport system for London – the underground railway. Of course, this is for steam trains.

11 January 29 BC
Rome, Italy. Augustus takes over complete control of the Roman Empire. He's a bit of a coward who wears a sealskin coat to protect him from lightning. Shocking.

12 January 1950
River Thames, England. 'Truculent' means fierce. Someone decided it would be a good name for a British submarine. But today HM submarine *Truculent* bumps into a ship – fiercely enough to sink them both. Sixty-four people die.

13 January
St Hilary's Day. Hilary is a fella, by the way. This is supposed to be the coldest day of the year so St Hilary ought to be the patron saint of thermal underwear.

14 January 1976
Long Island, USA. George Lutz and his family leave their home for good. But they've only lived there 28 days. They've been driven out by a curse, by nightmares, by pigs peering in at the windows, horrible smells, blood-soaked walls, a ghostly white figure and green slime that slithers down the stairs to get them. This will be known as the Amityville Horror … but is it just a horrible fake?

15 January 1919
Boston, USA. Disaster strikes in a strange and terrible way. A storage tank bursts and 21 people are drowned … in nearly

5 million litres of black treacle. (No jokes, please, about them coming to a sticky end.)

16 January 1920
USA. Great idea. Today is the last day before drinking alcohol in the whole country is banned. It's called 'prohibition'. But people who want to keep drinking pay lots of money for secret supplies. Lots of money attracts lots of gangsters who have booze made and delivered. They don't care if they murder each other (as well as assorted policemen and innocent citizens) to make their fortunes. The Gangster Age is born. Rotten idea leads to lots of horrible deaths.

17 January 1899
New York, USA. Gangster Al Capone is born today. Little does anyone know that he will have a very happy 21st birthday (1920, you dummy) because today's prohibition laws allow Big Al to become the world's most famous gangster, nicknamed 'The Big Shot'. He once killed three men with a baseball bat but ended up in prison for not paying his taxes.

18 January 1890
Turin, Italy. King Amadeo dies where he was born. But he isn't the king of Italy – he's the king of Spain. And not very popular there, where they called him 'The Intruder King'. The Spanish made his life a misery by laughing at the way he and his wife dressed. (They probably had the clothes sense of a pair of teachers.)

19 January 1915
Great Yarmouth, England. A German airship appears over the town and drops bombs which kill innocent Brits. This has never happened before so the proud people of Yarmouth become a famous first. Of course, some of them are too dead to enjoy their moment of glory.

20 January 1936
London. King George V dies ... with a little bit of help from his doctor. He was dying anyway, and the waiting 'just exhausts the onlookers and keeps them strained' (the royal doctor wrote). Quick injection of morphine and it's 'Goodnight George'. In fact the doctor murdered the king.

21 January
St Agnes' Day. Little 12-year-old Agnes was a Christian so the Romans executed her. She was beheaded, or burned, or strangled, depending on which story you like best. BUT the legend says that any man who touched her turned blind. So, the mystery is, how did they manage to execute her?

22 January 1901
London. Queen Victoria dies today, after a record 63 years on the throne. Still, she should have died almost 60 years ago. In 1842 John Francis shot at her as she drove past in her carriage, then he ran away. Amazingly, Vic agreed to go back next day to give Francis a second chance – that way the police could grab him. Sure enough Francis tried again and

was arrested. Francis was not executed, however, and this left the queen un-amused.

This 'popular' lady survived six other assassination attempts:

<u>10 JUNE 1840</u>
Edward Oxford
Two loaded pistols – missed

<u>3 JULY 1842</u>
John William Bean
Pistol – loaded with paper

<u>19 MAY 1849</u>
William Hamilton
Fired pistol – no bullet

<u>27 JUNE 1850</u>
Robert Pate
Hit with brass head
of walking stick

<u>29 FEB 1872</u>
Arthur O'Connor
Pistol – not loaded

<u>2 MARCH 1882</u>
Roderick McLean
Revolver – missed

23 January 1556
Shensi, China. Some people believe that the world is balanced on the back of a tortoise. When the tortoise moves the earth trembles – this is what causes an earthquake. (You can believe this if you wish.) In China on this day an earthquake kills 830,000 people – possibly the worst earthquake ever. A turtle disaster, in fact.

24 January

Britain. Paul's Pitcher Day. Cornish tin-miners celebrate St Paul's Day by putting an empty beer pitcher on the ground. They throw stones at it until it is wrecked. They then replace it with a full one. After drinking the beer they start again ... and again. Not a lot of tin is mined on this day.

25 January 1759

Alloway, Scotland. Scottish poet Robert Burns is born. He goes on to write 'To A Mouse' and 'To A Haggis' – sadly neither the mouse nor the haggis reply.

26 January 1788

Sydney, Australia. Britain has solved its over-crowded prisons problem. Take the convicts and dump them on a huge continent on the other side of the world. The first convicts arrive today.

27 January 1926

London. A Scottish inventor called Baird demonstrates a fiendish new machine that will change the lives of millions of people. It will allow untold terrors into the ordinary living room. It will turn a sane person brain dead after just a few hours. It may well have turned you brain dead – just you're too brain dead to notice. That's right, it's a thing called ... 'television'.

28 January 1829
Edinburgh, Scotland. Record crowds of 25,000 gather for the public hanging of body snatcher William Burke. He and his partner, William Hare, murdered the poor and lonely of Edinburgh and sold the bodies to the surgeons for students to practise on. A grave offence.

29 January 1820
England. King George III dies today. Some people say he became ill from drinking lemonade from a lead bowl. George is deaf too, but he should have known that hearing aids are safer than lemonades. Here are some of Georgie's unusual habits:

He sometimes ended every sentence with the word 'peacock'.

Believed London was flooded and ordered a yacht.

Wore a pillowcase around his head and tried to adopt a pillow as a son.

Believed he had actually died and wore black mourning clothes out of respect.

30 January 1649
London. Charles I goes for the chop. He wears two shirts because he doesn't want to shiver and for people to think he is afraid. He will end up very cold, of course.

31 January 1788
Rome, Italy. Bonnie Prince Charlie dies. He was the grandson of King James II who was thrown off the throne. Charlie once invaded Britain to take the throne but ended up defeated and having to run away to Rome.

CONSCRIPTION STARTS TODAY IN BRITAIN
– 9 FEBRUARY 1916

FEBRUARY

1 February 1851
England. Writer Mary Shelley dies. Her most famous creations are Doctor Frankenstein and his monster made up of bits of human beings. Of course the monster turns on Frankenstein and he says, 'The beauty of the dream vanished and breathless horror and disgust filled my heart.' So don't go trying to build a monster in your science lessons.

2 February
USA. Groundhog Day. It is said that the little ratty groundhog sleeps through the winter then pokes its nose above the ground today. (Where does it buy an alarm clock that rings once a year?) If it's a dull day, and the creature cannot see its shadow, then it's time to wake up. But if it's a clear day then there will be six more weeks of cold weather, so it goes back to bed.

3 February 1160
Crema, Italy. Emperor Barbarossa has had the city of Crema under siege for six months. 'I have Crema children as prisoners.' he announces. 'I will place them in my war catapults and fire them at your city walls,' he threatens. No one would be that cruel, would they? No one except Barbarossa. Splat. Splat. Splat.

4 February 1953
England. After the Second World War there was a shortage of sweets and they have been on 'ration' for ten years. Today is the last day of sweet rationing. Tomorrow you can go out

and buy all you can afford, make yourself sick, rot your teeth, grow larger than a poisoned pig and have a heart attack. At least cigarettes give a health warning on the packet before they kill you.

5 February 1788

England. Robert Peel is born today and invents the police force in 1829. They are nicknamed 'Peelers' or 'Bobbies' after Bob Peel. Everyone thinks they are government spies and hates them at first. Children jeer at the police with a rhyme: 'I spy blue, I spy black. I spy a Peeler in a shiny hat'. This also warns criminals that a policeman is in the area.

6 February 1918

Britain. Women are allowed to vote in elections from today – so long as they are over 30. It's taken a lot of fighting to get this right. The suffragettes chained themselves to railings, fought with police, and starved themselves on hunger strikes.

7 February 1301

Wales. King Edward I kills off the Welsh princes then gives the job, Prince of Wales, to baby son Edward. The Welsh don't want an English-speaking prince so the king pops baby Ed on a shield and shows him to the people. 'There you are.' he cries. 'A Prince who doesn't speak a word of English.' Great story – probably totally untrue.

8 February 1587
Fotheringay Castle, England. Mary Queen of Scots is executed for plotting against Elizabeth I. To prove she is dead the executioner picks up the head by the hair – and drops the head. No one told him that Mary wore a wig.

9 February 1916
Britain. It's the First World War and the posters say 'Your Country Needs You'. From today they should add, '... and we're coming to get you.' because 'conscription' is beginning. You now have a choice: go and be shot at by the Germans – or refuse, and be sent to prison by the British.

10 February 1850
Cape Horn, South America. A stone is carved in memory of 25-year-old William Kirkwood. He climbed to the top of the mast to spot whales. He fell off on this day in 1850. The verse says, 'The sea curls o'er him and the foaming billow, As his head now rests upon a watery pillow.' (In other words his body is still sloshing around in the South Atlantic.)

11 February 1466
Westminster Palace, London. Elizabeth of York is born, daughter of King Edward IV. Princesses like this are useful to big Ed – he can offer her hand (and the rest of her) in marriage as part of a treaty with some lord or other. Poor Liz is offered to three fellas before she ends up with Henry VII and becomes the mum of Horrible Henry VIII.

12 February 1554
London. Former queen, Lady Jane Grey, goes to her execution. Nicknamed the 'Nine Days Queen', Jane ruled as Queen of England from 10 July 1553 until she was overthrown by her cousin Mary I on 19 July. She found her nine days on the throne so stressful, that her skin actually started peeling off.

13 February 1866
Missouri, USA. The James gang take a bit of a liberty and attack a bank in the town of Liberty. In 1882 Jesse James is shot by someone claiming a $10,000 reward for his death. The gunman claimed to be his cousin.

14 February 1779
Sandwich Islands. Captain James Cook has sailed around the world twice and discovered Australia – though the Indigenous people may tell you it was never lost. On this day he takes part in a St Valentine's Day massacre. Some natives of the Sandwich Islands have taken the rowing boat from his ship Discovery. In the fight Captain Cook is killed. (Too many Cooks spoil the Sandwiches anyway.)

15 February 1898
Battleship Day, USA. Today we remember US battleship *Maine* – blown up in Havana Harbour. Very suspicious. US sailors vow revenge with a cry of 'Remember the *Maine*'. So US comedians invent a joke about a horse having its tail trimmed and crying, 'Remember the mane.' (Warning: laughing too hard can damage your health.)

16 February
St Juliana's Day. Lots of saints suffered terrible tortures but Juliana's was a bit over the top. She refused to marry a bloke so he had her roasted in flames, then dipped into boiling oil before finally being beheaded. Being a saint can be tough at times.

17 February 1598
Moscow, Russia. Boris Goudonov takes over as Tsar. ('Are you good enough?' the people cry. 'No I'm Goudonov,' he calls back.) He probably had Prince Dmitri murdered but that was seven years ago. Forgive and forget, eh?

18 February 1516
Greenwich Palace, London. Mary Tudor is born – known to her friends as 'Bloody Mary' because of her habit of burning Protestants. Her husband, King Philip of Spain probably thinks of her as 'Smelly Mary' – an illness makes the air from her nostrils stink. He leaves her and she becomes a miserable Mary.

19 February 1878
USA. Thomas Edison invents the 'phonograph' – a thing to record and play back music. Parents may like to blame him for the awful noises coming from their kids' bedrooms.

20 February 1513
Rome, Italy. Pope Julius is dead so he never gets to see the painting of the ceiling of the Sistine Chapel in Rome by Michelangelo. The picture is of God's creation of the world. God finished that job in six days, of course, but Michelangelo has been working for four years. He's been flat on his back in the locked room – a pain in the neck. He was also nagged by Pope Julius to 'hurry up' – and that's a real pain in the neck.

21 February 1437
Scotland. James II becomes king of Scotland. But these are troubled times and it's fight, fight, fight. Of course, he has some of those new 'cannon' things to help him at the siege of Roxburgh in 1460. Trouble is, the cannon explodes and blows James's leg off and that leads to his death. He's hopped the twig.

22 February 1968
Scotland. Farmer Steven Coyne, his son and his dog go out for a walk by their local lake. The dog barks furiously at a 4-metre slug with a long neck and a shiny black skin. The eyeless monster opens its mouth and swims towards the dog. They flee and report what they have seen ... another strange sighting in their local lake – Loch Ness.

23 February 1820
London. A group of men plot to kill the top members of Parliament: they are known as the 'Cato Street Conspiracy'. They think they can cut off the heads and stick them on Westminster Bridge. But unlike Guy Fawkes and the

rest of the 1605 plotters, the Cato Street leader, Arthur Thistlewood, and his conspirators are often forgotten. 'Penny for the Arthur' doesn't sound quite right.

24 February AD 303

Roman Empire. Emperor Diocletian begins the deadliest killing spree of Roman history: the persecution of Christians. Churches were shut down, and all Christian texts were burned. This bloodbath lasted for nine long years.

The Romans enjoyed watching people fight – fight each other to the death, or fight animals. Lots of action. Lots of blood. Lots of pain. But they also liked a bit of a change – two men with swords and shields all the time would be boring. So the weapons and the fights chopped and changed – while the fighters just chopped and dropped. Here are the main types of gladiators.

Key ⚔ Weapon 🛡 Armour

ANDABATAE
⚔ short sword
🛡 visored helmet with no eye holes, mail armour for limbs, chest and back plate

DIMACHAERUS
⚔ two swords

EQUESTRIAN
⚔ spear, sword
🛡 helmet, full tunic with arm guard, shield

HOPLOMACHUS
⚔ spear, sword
🛡 large helmet, round shield, complete suit of armour

LAQUEARIUS
⚔ noose
🛡 helmet, arm guards, leg guards

MURMILLO
⚔ sword
🛡 visored helmet with crest, oblong shield, arm, shoulder and leg guards

PAEGNIARIUS
⚔ whip, club
🛡 shield

PROVOCATOR
⚔ sword
🛡 visored helmet, curved shield, breastplate, arm and leg guards

RETIARIUS
⚔ trident, net
🛡 shoulder plate, arm guard

SAMNITE
⚔ sword
🛡 crested helmet with visor and plume, rectangular shield, arm and leg guards

SECUTOR
⚔ sword
🛡 round helmet with eye holes, oblong shield, arm and leg guards

THRACIAN
⚔ curved short sword
🛡 broad-rimmed helmet, small square shield, arm and leg guards

25 February 1634

Bohemia. An assassin bursts into warlord Von Wallenstein's bedroom and kills him on the orders of the Emperor. Nasty Von Wallenstein hated loud noises and ordered any dog to be killed if a bark disturbed him. Von Wall feels ruff now.

26 February 1815

Elba. The Brits were ever so pleased that they'd caught French leader Napoleon Bonaparte and stuck him on this island of Elba. But today he escapes. Somebody must have forgotten to lock the island. He gets back to France and stirs up trouble again.

27 February 1881

Majuba Hill, South Africa. Brit General George Colley camps his troops on top of Majuba Hill. The enemy 'Boers' set out to drive them off. When General George gets his head out of bed it is promptly hit by a bullet from a 12-year-old Boer.

28 February 1574
Mexico. The Spanish Inquisition sets out to find Protestants and convert them to being Catholics. Today they catch their very first Protestants in America. Some men are given 300 lashes and three become the first people to be burned at the stake on the American continent.

29 February 238 BC
Egypt. A year isn't 365 days long – it's 365 days, 5 hours 48 minutes and 45.5 seconds. King Ptolemy III orders that an extra day should be added to every fourth year, and the fantastic Pharaoh has created the first 'leap year'.

MARCH

1 March

Today is St David's day. St David is the patron saint of Wales – that's the country, not the whales that live in the sea. Today you should wear a leek and a daffodil (one in each ear looks very attractive). St David suggested that Welsh warriors should wear leeks in their hats so they'd know a fellow Welshman when they saw him on the battlefield and not kill him by accident.

2 March 1716

London. Sir Edmund Halley is well known for his astronomy. He gave his name to Halley's Comet – and the comet never said thank you. But this month Halley sees a brightly lit object hovering in the sky. The great astronomer says it isn't a star. So what is it? A very early UFO – or a glow-worm in his telescope?

3 March 1847

Scotland. Alexander Graham Bell is born. The man who grew up to invent the telephone – a machine that waits until you're in the bath before it decides to ring. Alexander's mum and his wife are not bothered by this – they are both deaf.

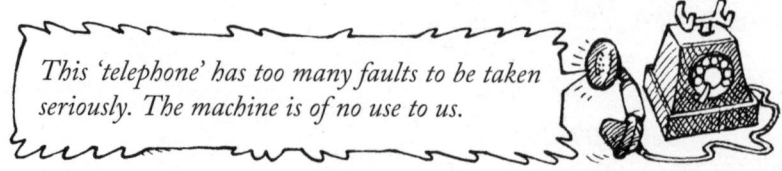

This 'telephone' has too many faults to be taken seriously. The machine is of no use to us.

4 March 1890
Scotland. At last the Forth railway bridge is opened. It's the longest in Britain at 8,093 feet. (In metres that's … er … a lot.) The old joke is that no sooner do they finish painting it than they have to start again at the other end. We forget that 73 people died building the bridge. And that's no joke.

5 March 1934
Texas, USA. Mother-in-law Day … at least that was the idea. The editor of a Texas paper suggests it for this day but it proves as popular as a 'Let's Club Baby Seals to Death Day'. Still, mothers-in-law everywhere look forward to gifts of flowers and chocolate and perfume. They may not GET them, but they can look forward to them.

6 March 1836
Alamo Fort, USA. A Mexican army attacks the Alamo Fort and kills every one of the 180 American defenders. The Mexican 'winners' managed to lose over 600 men, so who won? The answer is American writers and film-makers who had a great story to tell for the next 200 years. The American revenge is quick and deadly: their army catch the Mexican army napping – literally, because they were having their afternoon snooze. They kill 630 in the 21 April Battle of San Jacinto that lasts just 18 minutes.

7 March 1809
La Haye, France. Jean Pierre Blanchard dies. He was the first man to cross the English Channel by air – in a balloon.

Unfortunately, his balloons become his downfall, when he has a heart attack and falls over 50 feet during one of his flights. He survives the fall, but eventually dies from his injuries. The sky really was the limit.

8 March 1711
London. A French and English spy Antoine de Guiscard fails to murder the English Chancellor of the Exchequer Robert Harley. Harley's survival was thanks to his ornate waistcoat, which protected him from Guiscard's penknife. Unfortunate Guiscard suffered more bad luck, as he ended up losing his life due to injuries sustained in the fight.

9 March 1566
Edinburgh, Scotland. A murderous merry-go-round starts. Mary Queen of Scots has a favourite musician called David Rizzio and today her jealous husband has him murdered. But, within a year, Mary's husband dies when his house is blown up. Mary marries the man who probably killed her husband.

10 March 1873
Kansas, USA. Doctor York tells his friends that he is going to the Bender family's inn for a meal on his way home. But Doctor York is never seen alive again. The friends search for him and the Benders tell them that York must have been attacked after he left them. But when the friends go back, the bloodthirsty Bender family has fled ... leaving 12 'guests' behind – under the floor. The Benders are never caught.

11 March 1987

Britain. National No Smoking Day. This campaign is organised by Action on Smoking and Health – ASH. But they're a week too late. Last Wednesday was Ash Wednesday. They say today's a great success and 50,000 have given up smoking. They don't say how many have taken it up.

12 March 1609

Bermuda. The island of Bermuda becomes a British colony on this day. But would the Brits take it over if they knew about the dreaded 'Bermuda Triangle'? An area where ships and planes and people disappear without trace, without a sound and sometimes without their breakfast.

13 March 1881

St Petersburg, Russia. At a parade a terrorist throws a bomb under Tsar Alexander II's carriage. A man calls, 'Are you hurt, your majesty?' Alexander says, 'Not at all, thank God.' The man chucks a second bomb at him. 'Home to the palace to die.' Alex cries. And that's where his guards take the bits.

14 March 1757

Portsmouth, England. Admiral John Byng was given the job

of leading British ships to the island of Minorca to fight the French. He failed ... so today he is shot by a firing squad. Bang-byng.

15 March 44 BC

Roman leader Julius Caesar goes to the Senate even though he's poorly – his wife and a fortune-teller both warned him not to go. At the Senate a friend tries to hand him a warning note. Twenty-seven other 'friends' get their knives in first.

Caesar is very poorly by the time they've finished with him.

16 March AD 37

Capri. Emperor Tiberius stops breathing and is declared dead ... then he sits up and demands food. Young Caligula is waiting for old Tiberius to die so he can take over as emperor – so Tiberius is smothered with his own bedclothes. And this time he really IS dead.

Caligula ruled the Roman Empire from AD 37–41...

* He thought he was god.
* His girlfriend was his sister.
* He had people executed for fun.
* He made his horse a consul*.

*Or did he? This is a popular story about Caligula. But the *Horrible Histories* truth is Caligula SAID he could make his horse Incitatus a consul (Roman official) but never did. It was probably his idea of a joke.

17 March
St Patrick's a Brit who was sold to Ireland by slave traders. What does he think of his new country? Not a lot – he runs away to France. But, he goes back to Ireland later, converts them to Christianity and drives all the snakes out of Ireland in his spare time. So, the Irish forgive him. They even make him their patron saint.

18 March AD 978
Corfe Castle, England. 16-year-old King Edward comes to see his mum. Soldiers stab him then tie his foot to his horse's stirrup and watch as he's dragged to death. Most people reckon the one who gave the order for Edward's murder is … his mum. No Mother's Day card for her this year.

19 March 1950
USA. Edgar Rice Burroughs dies. (No relation to Edgar Rice Pudding.) Burroughs created the famous character Tarzan. No more Tarzan stories – no more awful jokes like, 'What's Tarzan's favourite Christmas song?' 'Jungle Bells.' (Groan.)

20 March 1413
Westminster Abbey, London. King Henry IV was quite

sure that he would die in Jerusalem. Rather wisely he kept away from that city – wouldn't you? But today he goes to Westminster Abbey and enters the Jerusalem Chamber … where he has a stroke and dies. Life plays funny tricks like that (though it wasn't so funny for Henry, of course).

21 March 1556
Oxford, England. Thomas Cranmer was the first Protestant Archbishop of Canterbury. But now Catholic Mary's on the throne and Thomas is in hot water – to be exact he's in hot fire when he is burned at the stake today.

22 March 1979
India. Jayaprakash Narayan is one of India's most loved and respected old leaders. Imagine the sadness when his death is announced this morning. Imagine the astonishment when Jayaprakash Narayan turns on the radio and hears about his own death. This false alarm came from the Director of India's Intelligence Department. Not all THAT intelligent then.

23 March
St Gwinear's Day. But it doesn't pay to follow this Irish saint. He took 770 men and women to Wales and Brittany to preach and some of them came to very nasty ends. King Teudar of Cornwall threw them into a lake full of poisonous snakes. The local newspaper could have announced, '770 Saint's Supporters are Snakes' Snacks.'

24 March 1956

Aintree, England. A dramatic Grand National horse race. The Queen Mother's horse, Devon Loch, is heading for the first royal win of this century. Suddenly it sprawls on the ground, staggers back to its feet ... and loses. A complete mystery. The sort of mystery that bestselling author Dick Francis could have written a book about. He should have, because he was riding Devon Loch at the time.

25 March 1911

New York, USA. Tragedy when fire destroys a clothes factory. The girls who aren't burned are killed when they jump from the windows on to the pavement below, many of them still clinging on to their pay packets.

26 March 1964

London. The trial of the 'Great Train Robbers' is over. They stole a couple of million pounds from a train. The judge decides to make an example of them so his sentences are harsh. Murderers usually get 20 years – the robbers get 30.

27 March 1905

London. Alfred and Edward Stratton break into a shop ... a common enough crime, but they break straight into the record books. The crime is solved by fingerprint evidence – for the first time in history. This is no comfort to the shopkeeper who dies in the raid.

28 March 1938
Borley, England. In England's most haunted house, Borley Rectory, a ghost announces, 'The house will burn down this very night.' The spirit, called Sunex Amures, obviously didn't own a diary because he got it wrong – by 11 months. It actually burned down on 27 February 1939.

29 March 1461
Towton, England. The Yorkists fight the Lancastrians in what is said to be the bloodiest battle ever fought on British soil. Men march over a carpet of dead bodies and through driving snow. Up to 28,000 die. The field where the battle was fought is still called 'Bloody Meadow' over 560 years later.

30 March 1867
Alaska. William Seward buys Alaska. That's right – the whole lot. He was sent from the USA to buy it from Russia. Everyone laughed – especially the Russians. Then gold is discovered. Will has the last laugh and laughs longest.

31 March 1889
Paris, France. A 300-metre tall lump of metal called the Eiffel Tower is stuck up to celebrate the Universal Exhibition in Paris. Within 100 years the tower will be sold at least three times as scrap metal by clever tricksters to idiot buyers.

PERILS AT SEA

APRIL

1 April

Are you a 'gowk'? Maybe you're a 'cuckoo' or even an 'April Fish'? These are all names given to people who are fooled on 1 April. (In Britain you're an 'April Fool' of course.) Also called 'Noddy Day' by some people. Writer Mark Twain said, 'This is the day when we are reminded of what we are on the other 364 days.'

2 April

Kircaldy, Scotland. Taily Day. After April Fool's Day comes this jolly joke day for some Scots children. They try to pin tails to people's backs with messages on them like 'Kick me' or 'Kiss me quick'. Warning: do not try this on someone unless (a) they like a joke, and (b) they're smaller than you.

3 April 1367

England. Henry IV is born and grows up to be England's most miserable king. Henry suffered an illness like leprosy. A monk said, 'He was tormented for five years by a rotting of the flesh, by a drying up of the eyes and by a rupture of the intestines.' He also had so many lice on his head that his hair dropped out. That's lousy luck – hair today, gone tomorrow.

4 April 1968

Tennessee, USA. Martin Luther King tried to kill himself twice when he was 12 years old. He jumped out of his bedroom window. Today, he is a 39-year-old, famous for fighting for the rights of Black Americans. He steps on to the balcony of his hotel room and he is shot dead.

5 April 1242
Lake Peipus, Russia. A German army tries to invade Russia but comes to an icy end on the frozen Lake Peipus. (It's a bit like the Winter Olympics but with sword blades instead of ice-skate blades.) Strangely enough in exactly 700 years' time, another German army commanded by Adolf Hitler will try to attack the Russians, and will be beaten by the freezing conditions.

6 April 1909
North Pole. US hero, Robert E Peary, claims to have become the first man to reach the North Pole, although a later expedition says he could have been 50 miles from his target. Everyone forgets that Black American Matthew Henson was with him. On 6 April 1988 Henson's body is moved to a hero's grave.

7 April 1739
York, England. The famous highwayman Dick Turpin is hanged today. He was arrested for shooting a chicken, but nobody knew he was the famous thief. His old teacher recognised his handwriting and betrayed him. Would your teacher do that to you?

8 April AD 217
Rome. Emperor Caracalla is stabbed to death ... but don't feel too sorry for him. He shared the empire with brother Geta until he had Geta's throat cut as he ran to their mother's arms for protection.

9 April 1747

London. Eighty-year-old Baron Lovat is the last man to be publicly beheaded in Britain. He is executed for treason. So many people turn up to watch that a stand collapses and kills 20 spectators. This gives Baron Lovat a good laugh. But the man with the axe has the last laugh.

CHOPPING LIST

Not everyone is lucky enough to lose their head with a single chop. Sometimes bungling beheaders have bodged the butchery. Here are a handful of horrible hackings...

VICTIM	CRIME	EXECUTIONER	NUMBER OF CHOPS	WEAPON USED
Lord Balmerino	Fighting for Scotland against England, 1745	John Thrift – a very nervous man. He was so shaky, he needed wine to give him courage	3	axe
Rasmussen	Danish highwayman, 1887	The executioner was very drunk and made a mess of it. The crowd were so disgusted, Denmark never used beheading again.	3	axe
Henri Coiffier	French traitor, 1642	The executioner had never done it before and Coiffier nagged him to get on with it.	11	sword
Angelique Ticquet	French woman had old husband murdered, 1657	Sanson and son. Old Sanson couldn't kill the beautiful woman and left it to his son. As he was swinging she started chatting and he missed.	5	sword
Countess of Pole	Mother of an English traitor, 1541	Young assistant executioner – his boss, Cratwell, was on holiday. Old Countess was awkward and played 'catch me if you can'.	11+	axe

10 April 1336

Uzbekistan, Asia. Tamerlane is born. When he grows up he will be a powerful ruler, loving arts, learning, religion, chess ... and mass destruction. Enemy towns are given a choice: surrender now and be spared, or keep fighting and be massacred. One city hesitates so he attacks it, cuts off 30,000 heads then has fun arranging them in a pile in the marketplace.

11 April 1865

USA. The American Civil War ends today. President Abraham Lincoln has led the North to a victory over the South. But one southern supporter is a very bad loser. He's an actor called John Wilkes Booth and in three days' time he will shoot Lincoln ... in a theatre, of course.

12 April 1861

Fort Sumter, USA. Americans go to war today – against the Americans. In the next four years, more than a million Americans will be killed or wounded in the American Civil

War – North against South, often brother against brother. Many will die in vicious battles – but four times as many will die from hunger and disease.

13 April 1919
Amritsar, India. Many Indians object to the British running their country – Britain has enough trouble running Britain. The Indian people hold a demonstration today and the Brit Army commander, Brigadier Dyer, decides to put a stop to it. The official report at the time claimed that 379 Indian men, women and children stop protesting when the army shoots them dead. We know today that the actual number killed was much more.

14 April 1912
Atlantic Ocean. Captain Lord of SS *Californian* stops because of dangerous icebergs in the area. But another ship steams past him at full speed. 'Warn that ship of the danger.' Captain Lord tells his wireless operator. But the other ship doesn't listen. That ship is the *Titanic*. In the contest between the *Titanic* and an iceberg there is only going to be one winner. The ship went down through the night and eventually completely sank the next day.

15 April 1591
Scotland. The Earl of Bothwell is accused of trying to kill King James VI ... by witchcraft. Old Bothwell sent witches out to sea in a sieve to cause a storm to wreck James's ship. They did this by throwing bits of dead bodies into the sea. James, wisely, did not name his ship *Titanic* and he survives.

16 April 1850
London. The well-known model-maker, Madame Tussaud dies today. When the French Revolution started cutting noble heads off on the guillotine she had a cheerful little job. She picked up the heads and made a quick wax impression of the face before the victim was buried. Today Madame Tussaud's wax museum makes wax models of the rich and famous without waiting for their heads to be cut off.

17 April 1961
Cuba. A group of revolutionaries land at the Bay of Pigs and try to recapture their country of Cuba. With the help of the USA they should have won, but they make a bit of a pig's ear of the whole attempt. A Bay-of-Pig's ear, in fact.

18 April 1775
Lexington, USA. Paul Revere is famous for riding to Concord to warn the Americans that the British soldiers were attacking. The stirring tale is remembered in Longfellow's long poem about the midnight ride – except it isn't quite true.

Revere is arrested before he ever gets to Concord. Still, it's a shame to let the truth spoil a good story.

19 April 1587
Cadiz Harbour, Spain. English Captain Francis Drake has heard about Spain preparing a huge navy to attack England. Why hang around and wait for the attack? He sails to their harbour and sinks 30 large ships, dozens of small ones and ruins tons of supplies. Drake then ducks out.

20 April 1914
Ludlow, Colorado, USA. There have been 30 years of bitterness between coal miners and coalfield owners. The Ludlow miners are on strike so they have been thrown out of their houses and now live in tents. A gunfight breaks out with soldiers sent to drive the miners out. But, when the tents are burned, it's 13 sheltering women and children who die.

21 April 1918
France. Baron von Richthofen is a German ace fighter-pilot. His band of merry mid-air murderers are called von Richthofen's Circus. He rides around in a bright red plane, so everyone knows who he is: the Red Baron. Today he is finally shot down. No safety nets in this circus.

22 April

Nebraska, USA. Arbor Day. That's a day set aside for planting trees. In Nebraska it's a public holiday … why not tell your teacher you want a day off to plant a tree?

23 April 1564

Stratford, England. Britain's greatest playwright, William Shakespeare, is born on this day. He grows up to write comedies and tragedies. But the greatest tragedy is that he also dies on this day in 1616. Imagine that. He probably never even got to open his prezzies.

24 April

St Mark's Eve. Attention all unmarried women. Leave a flower in the porch of your local church, then go back after midnight and pick it up. You will not only see a wedding procession but will also see the ghost of your future husband. But who wants to marry a ghost anyway? Creepy.

25 April

Anzac Day. That's short for Australia and New Zealand Army Corps. In 1915, during the First World War, the Anzacs attack Gallipoli in Turkey. Half of the 400,000 attackers are killed or wounded over the next eight months of disaster.

26 April AD 121
Rome, Italy. Marcus Aurelius is born and will become Roman Emperor. His first act as emperor amazes everyone – he offers to share the empire with his brother. For the first time the Roman empire has two Caesars. Maybe they carved up the empire using a pair of Caesars. (Pair of scissors – geddit? Oh, never mind.)

27 April 1521
South America. Ferdinand Magellan sails round Cape Horn to be the first European to reach the Pacific Ocean after crossing the Atlantic. There will be just 15 survivors of the 265 who left Spain ... and old Ferdy won't be one of them. He is killed in a punch-up with a Pacific Island tribe. That's a nice death compared to the other two captains he beheaded (for mutiny), or the rest who starved, drowned in shipwrecks or died from diseases.

28 April 1789
Pacific Ocean. Cruel Captain Bligh is captain of *The Bounty* (the ship, not the chocolate bar). He is so nasty to his crew that today they pack him off in a lifeboat. Nasty Bligh survives an incredible 4,160 mile journey and lives to become Governor of New South Wales, Australia.

29 April 1916
Dublin, Ireland. Rebel Irish decide to stamp out British rule so they attack what? The Dublin Post Office, of course. Where else would you go for a stamp? When the British bring in the big guns the Post Office catches fire. In five days

450 are dead and 3,000 injured. That's what happens when you stick to your post.

30 April 1945
Berlin, Germany. Adolf Hitler married his girlfriend, Eva Braun yesterday. Today he shoots her then he shoots himself. Not so much a tragic death – more a tragedy that he was ever born. He led Germany into the Second World War. Britain and her allies (especially Russia) suffered enormous losses of over 50 million, while Germany and her allies lost 11 million. Six million Jews were killed in the Holocaust.

MAY

1 May

On this day you should stick a Maypole up on your village green and dance around it. If you haven't got a village green then a traffic island will do. This day is known as Dipping Day in Cornwall, when people collect dew water and sprinkle others for luck. Why not collect a bucketful for your favourite teacher?

2 May 1885

Africa. King Leopold of Belgium sets up the Congo Free State in Africa – but most of the people are not free. They are forced to work for the Belgians, carrying huge loads of ivory and rubber. The enslaved Congolese are chained by the neck and whipped. Those who rebel are killed and have their hands lopped off.

3 May 1938

Rome, Italy. The Italian dictator, Benito Mussolini, welcomes the German dictator, Adolf Hitler, to Rome. These two buddies have a lot in common – they're cruel, destructive and power mad for a start. Benito started young – he was expelled from school for stabbing another pupil in the bum.

4 May 1979

London. British politicians are nervous. The new prime minister enters Parliament carrying ... a handbag. That's right. This is Britain's first woman prime minister, Margaret Thatcher.

5 May 1291

Acre, Middle East. A year ago the drunken Crusaders murdered everyone in the city who looked like a non-Christian. On this day the Muslim army has recaptured Acre after a long siege. The Crusaders scramble for the boats to flee to safety. The ones who don't make it are sold and enslaved.

6 May 1937

New Jersey, USA. The giant German airship, the *Hindenberg*, is coming in to land when it suddenly bursts into flames and crashes to the ground. Around 35 die, yet an incredible 64 survive. But was it really an accident...?

7 May 1915

The Irish Coast. Twelve hundred men, women and children go to the bottom of the Atlantic when the liner *Lusitania* is sunk by a German submarine. One hundred and twenty-eight of the victims are American, pushing America into the First World War on Britain's side. The Germans say the *Lusitania* was carrying weapons to Britain – and they could be right.

8 May 1884

Missouri, USA. Harry S Truman's birthday. The US President is born on this day ... and is christened Harry S Truman a few days later. His two grandfathers were called Shippe and Solomon and both wanted Harry to be named after him. To keep them both happy the baby's parents gave him the middle name 'S' – just the letter.

9 May 1671
The Tower of London, England. A daring attempt to steal the Crown Jewels almost succeeds. Colonel Blood leads a gang of thieves who flatten the crown and try to saw the sceptre in half. When Blood is caught, King Charles II not only forgives him – he likes the man's cheek so much he gives him land and money.

10 May 1941
London. A German air-raid destroys the Houses of Parliament. Some unknown German pilot succeeds where Guy Fawkes failed. Of course, old Guy didn't have the Luftwaffe (the German air force) to help him.

11 May 1812
London. People keep assassinating American presidents, but today sees the only assassination of a British prime minister, Spencer Perceval. He is shot in Parliament by John Bellingham who blamed the government for his business being ruined. Bellingham is executed.

12 May 1310
France. The Knights Templars are sort of fighting monks. They are also very rich and King Philip the Fair fancies getting his hands on their money. He has the Knights Templars arrested and tortured till they admit terrible

crimes. This gives him an excuse to burn 54 of them at the stake on this day. As the Grand Master of the Templars dies he cries, 'God will avenge our deaths.' Sure enough, four years later Philip the Fair dies. Fair enough.

13 May 1787
Portsmouth, UK. The first ships carrying convicts are sent to the new land Captain Cook had 'discovered'... Australia. This particular ship had 717 convicts, including nine-year-old chimney sweep, John Hudson, and 88-year-old rag dealer, Dorothy Handland. The trip was around five months long, and passengers often died from disease on the journey.

14 May 1610
Paris, France. King Henry IV goes for a ride in his carriage and is caught in a traffic jam. Suddenly a mad monk called

Francois jumps on to the carriage and stabs the king. Henry dies crying, 'I have been stabbed.' As famous last words go these are pretty pathetic.

15 May 1536
London. Anne Boleyn, Queen of England, goes to trial on charges of treason, adultery, and incest. Who accused her of these crimes? Her loving husband, of course! Poor Anne is sentenced to be executed.

16 May 1943
Ruhr Valley, Germany. British inventor, Barnes Wallis, invents a new weapon. Today British bombers drop 'bouncing' bombs and smash German dams. They lose 300 million gallons of water. Warning: do not try this with a bar of soap in your bath.

17 May 1900
Mafeking, South Africa. A thousand British soldiers have been trapped in the town for seven months by the South African Boer Army. Today the town is 'relieved' by forces led by Robert Baden-Powell. He goes on to found the Boy Scouts – and many parents will be 'relieved' to get rid of their kids for a week's summer camp.

18 May 1980
Mount St Helens, USA. Everyone knew the volcano was going to blow – but 57 people die today when it finally does.

Instead of running away, they go to the mountain for a closer look. Curiosity killed the cat.

19 May 1606
Moscow. Phoney Tsar Dmitri is captured while escaping from the royal palace. (Since he breaks both his legs jumping from a window, it isn't too hard to capture him.) He is executed and cremated, then his ashes are blown from a cannon.

20 May 1588
Lisbon. The Spanish Armada of 132 ships sets sail to invade England. Only 60 will return. Final score: England 1, Spain 0. English Sea Captain Francis Drake is a real hero after this.

21 May AD 685
Northumbria, England. The great king of Northumbria, Ecgfrith, dies in a battle with the Picts from north of the border. Ecgfrith and his men follow the Picts into a narrow valley where they disappear into a mist. The road is blocked by a huge boulder. The Picts come out of the mist and annihilate the Northumbrians. One man escapes.

22 May 1915
Quintinshill, Scotland. A little local train stands at the platform. The signalman lets the Glasgow Express come through ... on the same line. He forgot about the local train. Crash number 1. The wreckage and survivors are scattered across the other line so when the 600-ton London Express arrives ... crash number 2. Hundreds die because of the signalman's slip of memory.

23 May 1618
Prague, Bohemia. The royal palace is attacked by a mob and three men are thrown out of a window. The first cries, 'Holy Mary. Help.' And she does. The three men land in a rubbish tip ... and live smellily ever after.

24 May 1964
Peru vs Argentina football match in Lima, Peru. An unpopular decision by the referee caused a riot which killed 300 and injured 500. The worst football disaster in history.

25 May AD 735

Jarrow, England. The monk-historian Bede dies today. He wrote long books with goose-feather pens on skin from the belly of a calf. (The calf was dead at the time.) Bede was superstitious and he heard reports that the moon turned the colour of blood and blood rained down from the skies. 'A sign that I will die soon,' he predicted. Raining blood is worse than raining cats and dogs.

Did you know that the phrase 'raining cats and dogs' comes from England in the 1600s? During heavy downpours of rain, many of these poor animals drowned. Their bodies could be seen floating in the rain that raced through the streets. It looked as if it had rained 'cats and dogs'.

26 May 1868

Newgate Prison, London. Michael Barrett goes down in history. Unfortunately he goes down with a rope round his neck when he becomes the last man to be executed in public in England. Michael probably doesn't enjoy his moment of glory. He's too upset – really choked in fact.

27 May 1818

New York, USA. Amelia Jenks Bloomer is born today.

She goes on to be a great fighter for women's rights. She gives lectures dressed in trousers tied at the ankle, worn under a short skirt. They become known as 'bloomers'. How would you like your name remembered as a piece of underclothing, like 'Jason Briefs' or 'Sharon Pants'?

28 May 1358
France. The French unpleasant peasants decide they've had enough and start hacking the nobles to pieces. These rebels are known as Jacquerie. Reports say they captured a knight, roasted him over a fire and forced his wife to eat the flesh. (She probably became a vegetarian after this.) The knights fight back, defeat the peasants – but don't eat them.

29 May 1651
England. This day sees celebrations for the escape of Charles II from Roundhead soldiers. Charles hid in an oak tree. In some villages children still wear oak leaves in remembrance today, which is known as Royal Oak Day.

30 May 1431

Paris, France. Joan of Arc led the French into battle against the English. Now she is finally captured, the English want rid of her for good. They can't murder a prisoner of war (it's not cricket). But they can try her as a witch. She is found guilty (surprise, surprise) and burned to death at the stake today. The English lose the war in the end, which serves them right.

31 May 1916

The North Sea. Some people call the naval fight which begins today at Jutland, 'the greatest sea battle in history'. The Germans say they've sunk the British – the British claim to have wiped out the Germans. Nobody has won – the dead are the real losers.

PERILS OF THE BATTLEFIELD

JUNE

1 June AD 1014

London. Viking raiders sack London. (No, that doesn't mean they throw it out of a job – they wreck it.) They attach ropes from London Bridge to their longboats, row away and, what do you think? London Bridge is falling down.

2 June 1567

Ulster, Ireland. Shane O'Neill has been fighting for control of Northern Ireland. Now people are fighting for control of his head (which is no longer attached to his shoulders, by the way). In a fight with his Scottish friends he is hacked to death. His English enemies get his head, pickle it and stick it on a pole on Dublin Castle walls where he has a lovely view.

3 June 1665

Lowestoft, England. The British Fleet is commanded by the Duke of York (later James II) and beats the attacking Dutch. Hard cheese, Dutch – or hard Dutch cheese, if you prefer.

4 June 1520

France. Fat Henry VIII of England meets skinny Francis I of France to sign a treaty and have a bit of a party. Henry said to Frank, 'Brother, we will wrestle,' knowing he should win. But little Frank used a cunning French trip to flatten Henry.

5 June 1893
Massachusetts, USA. 'Lizzie Borden took an axe, gave her mother forty whacks. When she saw what she had done, she gave her father forty-one.' That's what the old rhyme says. Lizzie's trial starts on this day ... but she is found not guilty (though everyone knows she did it). She lives comfortably on her murdered father's money. Who says 'Crime doesn't pay'?

6 June 1981
Near Mansi, India. A train driver brakes to avoid hitting a cow (sacred animals for Hindus). The train plunges off the bridge and between 250 and 500 are killed. The driver really should have told the cow to moo-ve.

7 June 1329
Scotland. The country is upset to learn that King Robert the Bruce has died. This heroic man won them their freedom ... and also murdered his rival John Comyn, had rebels executed and terrorised the people of northern England. Still, nobody's perfect.

8 June AD 632
Medina. The Prophet Mohammed dies today. He was not very fond of dogs – he said they were unclean – but he loved moggies. He once found a cat had fallen asleep on his sleeve. Rather than wake it up he cut off his sleeve and walked away. A gentle man – quite armless in fact.

9 June 1870

England. Popular writer Charles Dickens dies on this day. He suffered from insomnia – he couldn't sleep, no matter how many sheep he counted. He had to position himself exactly in the middle of the bed which was facing north. Maybe he should have slept on the very edge of the bed – that way he'd soon drop off.

10 June 1190

Asia Minor. Emperor Barbarossa is dead. He was happy to massacre children (see 3 February). Now he has set off on a Crusade to massacre a few thousand Turks and capture Jerusalem. But as he was crossing a river he fell off his horse. Heavy armour dragged him to the bottom. Glug. Glug.

11 June 1567

Edinburgh, Scotland. Edward McGregor is proud of his beard – believed to be the longest in the world. Unfortunately he steps on it as he is going down some stone steps and falls. Ed's dead. But, if he'd survived, would he have said, 'Och. That was a close shave'?

12 June 1667

Kent, England. Britain has always been proud of its navy – but not today. A Dutch fleet attacks and burns Sheerness town then wrecks British ships in their docks at Chatham. Worst of all they pinch the *Royal Charles* (the king's flagship) and sail back to Holland with it. The Dutch have *Royal Charles*, the Brits look like right royal charlies.

13 June 1381
London. Wat Tyler, leader of a Peasants' Revolt that beheaded a judge and a bishop, comes for peace talks with King Richard II. But Tyler is betrayed and now it's his turn to have his head cut off. The peasants go home after losing their head man (or head-less man).

14 June 1645
Naseby, England. Oliver Cromwell leads his New Model Army into their first battle against the Cavaliers – the King's army – and Cromwell wins. A historian of the time said that the Cavaliers 'fell like ripe corn around the King'. And the ones who survived had their noses slit by the enemy.

15 June 1215
Runnymede, England. A great day in English history and a pretty good day for the battling Barons of England. They make King John sign *Magna Carta* (Great Charter) which gives them lots of lovely power. It also promises justice to all free men. (Too bad if you're an enslaved person, of course.)

16 June 1487
Nottinghamshire, England. A young man called Lambert Simnel claims that he is in fact the true king. Henry VII gets fed up with Lambert and they meet in battle today. Lambert loses. Henry could execute him, but young Lambert is so pathetic Henry thinks of a more suitable fate – he gives Lambert a job, as a kitchen boy. Instead of getting the chop he gets the chops.

17 June 1775

USA. The Americans are revolting – against their British rulers. First major battle of the American Revolution today, known as the Battle of Bunker Hill – though it is actually fought at Breed's Hill nearby. Famous American order: 'Don't fire until you see the whites of their eyes.' The beaten Brits end up with blood-shot eyes.

18 June 1815

Waterloo, Belgium. This Waterloo is a village, not a railway station. Today Napoleon Bonaparte sees his army blown-apart by the Duke of Wellington and his army.

19 June 1536

London. King Henry VIII goes for a jolly game of tennis while it's game, set and match for his second wife, Anne Boleyn. The executioner has a neat forehand stroke that lops off her head.

20 June 1597

The Arctic. Dutch explorer Barents dies when his ship is trapped by ice. His men have survived polar bear attacks and lived by eating foxes. But, today, Barents finally freezes. The foxes probably enjoyed that.

21 June 1855

London. A grizzly group of ghosts told a doctor that he would die, on this day, in his haunted house in Portman Square. The doctor believes it is a fate he can't avoid. His friends find him – he has died of a heart attack. Gruesome.

22 June AD 304

St Alban's Day. Alban is sheltering a Christian priest when the Roman soldiers march in to search for the man. Alban pretends he is the priest. The Romans believe him ... and give him the chop. The priest is happy and free, the Romans are happy because they think they've got their man and Alban is happy because he's a martyr. Only God is unhappy. He makes the executioner's eyes fall out. Plop. Plop.

23 June AD 79

Rome, Italy. Emperor Vespasian dies today. He has started building the Colosseum but dies before it's complete. Poor Vesp will miss the deaths of 9,000 animals and 2,000 gladiators – and that was just in the first 100 days of its opening in AD 80.

24 June 1314

Bannockburn, Scotland. Edward II is hammered by the Scots today. His knights set off to swat the Scots. The Scots leader, Robert Bruce, is caught riding alone in front of his men. English knight Sir Henry de Bohun charges him with a lance to finish the fight in one mighty blow. Robert ruins the glorious charge ... he ducks. Then bashes Bohun's bonce.

25 June 1876
Dakota, USA. General Custer attacks an Indigenous American camp at the Little Bighorn. Little Big mistake, General. He is hopelessly outnumbered. Indigenous American warrior Standing Bear says later, 'There were so many of us that I think we did not need guns.' Custer and his men say nothing after the battle. They're all dead.

26 June 1483
England. Richard III comes to the throne – while his royal nephews disappear mysteriously from the Tower of London. Has Richard murdered them? Some say 'yes' and also accuse him of drowning his brother in a barrel of wine and poisoning his own wife. Others say it's all lies. A killer king? Or a misunderstood monarch? Who knows?

27 June 1844
Illinois, USA. Joseph Smith founded a religion known as the Mormons. He said he'd read a lost part of the Bible, written on gold sheets and buried in a hill near New York. The people who believed Joe Smith joined his church. The ones who didn't believe him beat him to death on this day.

28 June 1914
Sarajevo, Bosnia. Archduke Ferdinand of Austria is visiting the city and is greeted with an assassination attempt. Any need for extra guards for Ferdy's journey home? No one seems to think so, and of course the second attempt on his life succeeds. Oooops. This starts a

chain of events that will lead to the First World War and another 10 million deaths.

29 June 1613
London. Will Shakespeare's play 'Henry VIII' is performed at the Globe theatre. On to the stage strides the actor playing King Henry. A cannon fires blanks to greet him and sparks shower from its mouth. They set alight the thatched roof of the theatre. The only victim is a man who has his trousers set on fire but it's put out with a bottle of beer.

30 June 1470
Valois, France. Charles VIII of France is born. His death is simply tragic. The polite gentleman escorts his wife on to her tennis court. He is watching her and not the low roof, cracks his head on a beam and dies.

JULY

1 July 1916

The Somme, France. One of the bloodiest battles in history starts on this day. To inspire the East Surrey regiment their Captain Nevill has bought four footballs. He offers a prize to the first team to 'score' with a football in an enemy trench. Nevill is one of 19,000 killed in the first 30 minutes of the battle. Match abandoned.

2 July 1644

England. Battle of Marston Moor in the English Civil War. Cavalier leader Prince Rupert's white poodle is killed, and his black dog is captured by the enemy Roundheads. Their reporter writes, 'Our officers have cut the dog's ears and made him a Round Head.' (He no longer comes when they call, 'Ear, boy'.)

3 July 1844

Iceland. The last pair of Great Auks are killed. This bird was hunted to extinction for food and because its feathers made lovely fluffy mattresses. Alive yesterday, dead today, bed tomorrow.

Other animals that have gone extinct are...

Broad-faced Potoroo *Last seen: 1865, south-west Western Australia.* When convicts arrived from Europe they set about clearing the lands where the potoroo pottered about. With a name like that, it never had a chance.

Harpagornis *Last seen: around 1600, New Zealand.* This monster was the largest bird of prey ever known. It weighed 10 to 14 kg (31 lb) and attacked at speeds of up to 80 kmph (50 mph). The harpagornis lived in New Zealand and hunted moas. The Māori people killed off the harpagornis because it was a very dangerous monster to have in your skies. It was nicknamed the leopard eagle – it isn't spotted now.

Moa *Last seen: around 1600, New Zealand.* It was a grass-eater and pretty harmless (unless it sat on your bald head mistaking it for an egg). It was just a big fat dinner on legs. It couldn't fly so the Māori people (who arrived around AD 1000) killed off the moa for food. No more moa.

Tasmanian tiger *Last seen: 1933, Tasmania.* It wasn't even a tiger! But once dingoes arrived in Australia, the TT was driven out. It lived on in dingo-free Tasmania, but farmers killed it (to keep it from killing their cattle), hunters killed it (for a reward) and collectors collected it for zoos (because they thought they were 'saving' it – they weren't). Some people still say they see it today in Tasmania – and in Britain. (If that's true then someone should tell the TT it is very, very lost.)

Quagga *Last seen: 1883, Amsterdam, Holland.* The last one died on 12 August 1883 at the Artis Magistra Zoo. Its home was in South Africa. It looked like a zebra at the front and a horse at the back. Farmers killed it so it wouldn't eat their cattle's grass – and it made nice handbags too. Quagga just quit.

Lesser stick-nest rat *Last seen: 1933, Australia.* Once rabbits arrived in Australia they ate all the rat's grass. In 1859, 24 rabbits were set loose in Australia. Six years later there were two million. The lesser stick-nest rat just couldn't stick around after that.

Carolina parakeet *Last seen: 1918, USA.* The last one died in the Cincinnati Zoo. The trouble was it was just too pretty. The only parrot living in eastern USA, this parakeet was hunted to extinction for its feathers. (It also liked to nibble the farmers' crops.)

Passenger Pigeon *Last seen: 1914, USA.* The most amazing extinction of all because it was once the most common bird in the world. There were maybe five BILLION passenger pigeons in the USA. They lived in huge flocks of up to two billion birds. Such a flock would be a mile wide and 300 miles long, taking several days to pass. But the pigeon was hunted for food and numbers started to fall. Almost all of the remaining quarter-million passenger pigeons were killed in a single day in 1896 by sport hunters, who knew they were shooting the last wild flock. The last passenger pigeon, named Martha, died in the Cincinnati Zoo. Her stuffed body is on display at the Smithsonian Institution museum. As dead as a dodo...

Dodo *Last seen: 1681, Mauritius.* Once the Dutch settlers arrived, their rats and cats raided dodo nests. But the dodo was so friendly it stood still and let the Dutch smash its head and eat it, becoming extinct less than 80 years after the humans arrived. The dodo would not have won any beauty contests but it didn't deserve to dodo die. Now as dead as … a big-eared hopping-mouse.

4 July 1807
Italy. Giuseppe Garibaldi born. He grows up to be a rebel who will fight to make the states of Italy one country. Famous for saying, 'Rome or die.' Wins after many bloody battles and is a hero in Italy. of the name Garibaldi lives on … as a biscuit.

5 July 1865
Britain. The 'Red Flag Act' is passed today. It reduces the speed limit to 4 miles per hour and requires a man carrying a red flag to walk in front of the vehicle. In 1896 Walter Arnold speeds past a police station. A constable grabs his helmet and his bicycle and

gives chase. After five miles he catches him. Walter is the first motorist convicted for speeding. The fine is 5p.

6 July 1535
London. Sir Thomas More has upset his friend King Henry VIII and goes to his execution today. His head is boiled to preserve it then stuck on a pole on London Bridge.

7 July 1307
London. Edward I dies today. The king was so tall he was known as 'Longshanks' – a shank is another name for a leg. He ordered that, after death, his body should be boiled and his bones carried into battles against the hated Scots.

8 July 1884
England. National Society for the Prevention of Cruelty to Children is founded today. The good news is that neglected children can be helped. The bad news is that teachers will continue to beat kids with canes and straps for another 100 years, and the NSPCC don't seem to mind. Nowadays, teachers need an NSPCT – a National Society for the Protection of Cruelty to Teachers.

9 July 1727
Urbino, Italy. Saint Veronica Giuliani dies today. On Good Friday 1,697 wounds appear on her body, as if nails had pierced her hands and feet – what most people think of as Christ's wounds on the cross. But the truth is the Bible says he was stabbed in the side by a Roman soldier so he should have had FIVE wounds. So is Veronica a saint – or a fake?

10 July 1559
France. King Henry II has organised a great tournament. Of course, big-head Henry has to be the star. He smashes knight after knight but ends up with a lance in his head. Big-head becomes dead-head.

11 July 1099
Spain. The great warrior, El Cid, leads his soldiers to a glorious victory. Quite remarkable, since he is dead at the moment. His mummified body is strapped to a horse and sent on to the battlefield to encourage his men. Stuffed Cid stuffs enemy.

12 July 1794
Corsica. British Admiral Horatio Nelson loses his eye in the siege of Calvi. This is useful when he wants to ignore an order to retreat at Copenhagen five years later. He puts his telescope to his blind eye and says he can't see the signal. Strangely the Brit sea-hero loses an eye in a land battle and an arm at another land battle. He loses his life at sea, of course, so that's all right.

13 July 1793
Jean-Paul Marat, French Revolution leader is stabbed to death by Charlotte Corday while having a bath. For her crime she was sent to the guillotine, where the executioner snatched her dead head and punched it in the face.

14 July 1789
Paris, France. A mob of citizens attack the Bastille Prison and let the prisoners free ... all seven of them. They also pinch a supply of weapons, kill the governor and stick his head on a pole. This event is still celebrated today in France as the start of the French Revolution.

15 July 1869
France. Mix beef fat, skimmed milk and pork with flavourings and what have you got? Gut ache? No – 'margarine'. Napoleon III of France held a competition for inventors to come up with a cheap butter for the poor of France. The margarine produced on this day is white, greasy ... and a success. Urggggh.

16 July 1918
Ekaterinberg, Russia. The Russians were doing badly in the First World War so Tsar Nicholas II took command of the army ... and things got worse. The Russians blame Nick so they shoot him on this night. They also decide to blame his wife and children. This hardly seems fair, but they are shot too. It's tough at the top.

17 July 1453
Castillon, France. The English lose the battle of Castillon to the French and this brings an end to the Hundred Years War. It's been going on for 116 years. Clearly the 15th-century historians weren't very good at sums.

18 July 1762
Unpopular Tsar Peter III used to stick his tongue out at priests in church. Not anymore. Today he dies in a scuffle at the dinner table. But it probably wasn't an accident. Who arranged to assassinate him? His wife, Catherine the Great, who took the throne.

19 July AD 64
Rome, Italy. Emperor Nero (ruled AD 54–68) fiddles while Rome burns ... at least that's the popular story. Rumour says that Nero started the fire that devastates the city. Highly unlikely. He does, however, put tar-soaked leather jerkins on his enemies, stick them on poles and set fire to them as human torches. Nasty Nero ordered countless executions. He ends up being murdered himself.

Other things Nero did...

- Murdered his half-brother.
- Murdered his wife when he got a girlfriend, then kicked his girlfriend to death.
- Dressed up as a lion and attacked people at gladiatorial fights.

20 July 1969
The Moon. American astronaut Neil Armstrong becomes the first human to walk on the Moon. Neil finds it's not made of green cheese but grey sand. Unfortunately he left his bucket and spade back on Earth so he can't build a sandcastle. He has remembered the American flag and plonks it into the ground.

21 July 1518
Strasbourg, France. Ever danced until you dropped? The dancing plague took hold of hundreds of people, who danced uncontrollably for weeks, before stopping just as quickly and

mysteriously as it began. No one knows why, although some have blamed stress for the hysteria. Either that or some sort of poisoning from a botched batch of bread.

22 July 1934

Chicago, USA. John Dillinger makes a date with Anna Sage to take her to the cinema. Big mistake, John. He is a bank robber known as 'Public Enemy Number 1'. Anna tells the FBI where the gangster will be, and they fill him full of bullets as he leaves the cinema. Poor Anna has lost a boyfriend – but gained a $10,000 reward so she's not crying too much.

23 July 1478

Belgium. Philip the Handsome is born. After his death his wife keeps his corpse and sleeps with it beside her on the bed for three years. By this time Philip is no longer very handsome. His wife's name? Joanna the Mad. Guess why.

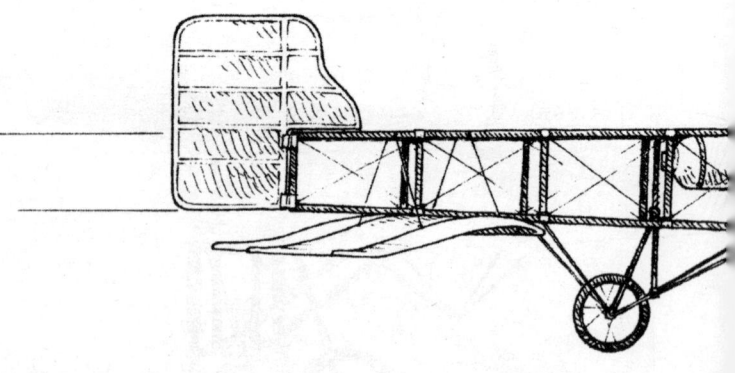

24 July 1505
Kilwa, East Africa. Portuguese sailor, Francisco de Almeida, arrives and expects King Ibrahim to welcome him. The King makes an excuse and doesn't turn up. Now de Almeida has an excuse – to shoot the Africans and take lots of precious loot.

25 July 1909
English Channel. Louis Bleriot is famous for being the first person to fly across water. He flew from France to England and his name went down in history. It was the most famous French landing since William the Conqueror landed at Hastings in 1066. But Bleriot should NOT have won the race to be first. He was just plain lucky. The *Daily Mail* newspaper ran a competition: £1,000 for the first pilot to fly across the Channel. The favourite to win the race was Frenchman Henry Latham, whose Antoinette plane had already broken records. How did Bleriot end up beating him? Latham forgot to set his alarm on the morning of the race, of course!

26 July
St Anne's Day. On this day girls should take a pod containing nine peas and place it on their doorstep. Put this message next to it: 'Come in my dear and do not fear.' The first man to enter the door will become your husband. (Warning: look through the letterbox before opening the door.)

27 July 1909
The Atlantic Ocean. A ship spots the SS *Waratah* heading for London. No one ever sees the *Waratah*, or the 211 people on board, again. But one man, Claude Sawyer, has dreamed about a bloodstained figure crying 'Waratah.' Cautious Claude saw this as a sign of doom and decided not to board the *Waratah*. He lived.

28 July 1540
London. Henry VIII marries his fifth wife, Catherine Howard. What he doesn't know is that young Cath had a few boyfriends before she met Henry. When he finds out he goes off his head with rage – in fact he goes, 'Off with Cath's head.'

29 July 1945
Pacific Ocean. Worst ever disaster for a US ship when the cruiser *Indianapolis* is hit by a Japanese torpedo and sinks. 800 survive the explosion but only 300 will be rescued five days later. Hunger and thirst kill a lot ... while the sharks make a picnic of the rest.

30 July 1863
USA. Henry Ford is born and goes on to make millions of cars which, strangely enough, are also called Fords. Unfortunately Henry has some wacky ideas, like making peace with his hero, Adolf Hitler. Then, during the Second World War, Henry built the bombers that finally flattened his hero.

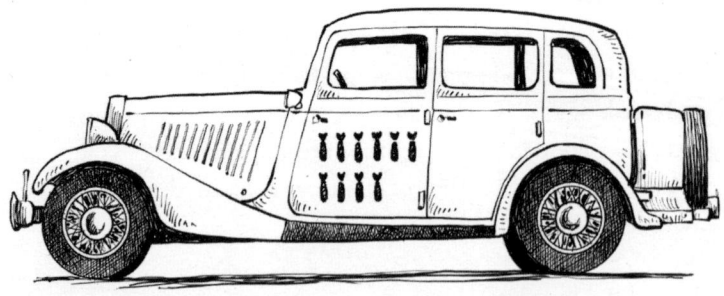

31 July 1910
Canada. The SS *Montrose* docks in Canada and a quiet little man called Doctor Crippen steps ashore. He is arrested. The Captain suspected that his passenger was a wanted man and radioed ahead for the police to be waiting. This is the first time wireless has been used in a murder hunt. Little Crippen has poisoned his wife, cut her into bits and buried the bits in the cellar of their home.

AUGUST

1 August 1978

A new law said New York City dog owners had to clean up after their pets. Before that about 41 million kilos of dog poo was left on the streets every year.

2 August 1274

Dover, England. New King, Edward I, comes home after a pretty good Crusade in Jerusalem. He made peace with the Muslims, but that didn't stop one of their groups, the 'Assassins', sending a killer after him. Anyway, lucky Ed survived the attack with a poisoned dagger.

3 August 1279

England. The English mop up after a huge storm that raged a day and a night causing floods and damage to crops. There is such a shortage of corn that the price goes up. King Edward complains that the palace cannot buy enough corn to make fresh bread. Poor King Ed – but imagine how much worse it is for the penniless peasants.

4 August 1265

Evesham, England. The revolting barons, led by Simon de Montfort, fight a royal army led by Prince Edward. De Montfort is cut into pieces. His head is sent to the wife of Roger Mortimer as a thank-you gift for helping to fight Simon. (Most of us would rather have a box of chocolates.)

5 August 1392

France. King Charles VI of France is riding with his guards when a leper leaps out and warns the king of a terrible 'doom'. Soon after this Charles's mental health suffers – something that doesn't stop him ruling the country, of course. Some unusual things Charles did were:

- He killed four of his own men with his sword.
- He imagined he was made of glass and would shatter if anyone touched him.
- He sometimes howled like a wolf.

6 August 1577

Oxford, England. A strange disease strikes down all the men who were in court a month ago. Women and children who were there are not affected. Judges, juries and criminals all die – 300 of them.

7 August 1840

Britain. Parliament passes a law banning the use of boys as chimney sweeps. Their bosses are upset, of course. They argue that the boys enjoy climbing through choking soot and fumes, scraping knees and elbows raw, choking to death when they get stuck and being beaten when they are careless. Quite right – no dead sweep boy has ever complained.

8 August AD 117
Roman Empire. Hadrian becomes Emperor today. He is famous for Hadrian's Wall and the ancient Roman joke about it – **Q:** Where is Hadrian's wall? **A:** At the bottom of Hadrian's garden.

9 August 1812
Barbados, Caribbean. It's Mr Thomas Chase's funeral today. The family pop him in a coffin and carry it down to the family vault where two of his children had already been buried. But, when the sealed door is opened the funeral party sees that his children's coffins have moved. How? No one will ever know.

10 August
St Lawrence's Day. Old Lawrence was tortured and executed for being a Christian but he was a pretty tough old cookie. He was roasted on a spit like a chicken. After a while he raised his head and said, 'Turn me over, please. I'm cooked on that side.'

11 August 1934
USA. A deserted American island full of sea birds is taken over and today it opens as a prison. It is called Alcatraz. You may escape the prison but you won't survive the swirling

currents and the freezing waters of San Francisco Bay. It is the world's toughest prison until it closes 29 years later.

12 August
Britain. The 'Glorious Twelfth' – the start of the grouse-shooting season. The grouse shooters try to shoot a 'brace' of birds. A brace is a pair. Dangerous sport because if they shoot four then they've shot a pair of braces ... and their trousers may fall down.

13 August 1756
Germany. Princess Adelaide is born. She grows up to marry King William IV of Britain. Their coronation is held at a time when the country is short of cash, and the coronation feast is scrapped. Adelaide even has to provide the jewels for her own crown. Still, it's all worth while when she has an Australian city named after her.

14 August 1900
Beijing, China. The Chinese Society of Righteous and Harmonious Fists (the 'Boxers' for short) has been making trouble. The Boxers have been murdering 'foreign devils' – lots of heads lopped off. But today the German, US and Brit foreign devils fight back and knock out the Boxers.

15 August 1057
Scotland. King Macbeth dies today. 550 years later everyone will remember him because William Shakespeare will write

a play about him. Unfortunately Will's quill makes Macbeth (and his lovely wife Gruach) into murderers. Macbeth killed the previous king in battle – not with a knife in the back as Shakespeare said.

16 August 1977
Tennessee, USA. Some people say that, on this day, pop singer Elvis Presley is found dead in the toilet. However, there have been thousands of sightings of Elvis, alive and well, in places from a Sacramento supermarket to a Chigwell chip shop. Thousands of people can't all be idiots, can they?

17 August 1982
Ayers Rock, Australia. Baby Azaria Chamberlain is tucked up in her bed in the family tent. But minutes later her mother cries, 'A dingo has got my baby.' The bloodstained clothes are found a week later – cut with a knife, not torn by a wild dog's teeth. The police arrest the baby's mother and it takes her six years to clear her name. But the mystery remains … who done it?

18 August 1587
First English child is born in America. She is called Virginia Dare. (No, stupid, her father is not the 1950s comic book space captain Dan Dare. How dare you even suggest it?)

19 August 1561
Leith, Scotland. Mary Queen of Scots returns from France to claim her throne. Elizabeth I of England has a group of

ships waiting to grab her and send her back throneless. But a mysterious fog descends and Mary gets through safely. (Don't worry, Liz will get her in the end. The neck end.)

20 August 1940
Mexico. The brutal Russian leader, Joseph Stalin, is afraid of Leon Trotsky. Trotsky hides in a fortress-house in Mexico but Stalin's assassins finally get close enough to kill him with an ice-pick in the head. Trotsky doesn't see the point.

21 August 1485
Leicestershire, England. King Richard III has some very nasty dreams. This is a bad sign, since tomorrow he has to meet Henry Tudor in battle at Bosworth Field. Richard has twice as many men as Henry, but sure enough the dreams were right and he ends up losing the battle and getting the chop.

22 August 1849
Venice, Italy. A famous first – the world's first bombers. The Austrians send hot-air balloons over Venice with 30-pound bombs attached. The bombs don't cause much damage. But in August exactly a hundred years later, Japan is dedicating the town of Hiroshima as a shrine of peace after a single nuclear bomb killed 130,000 people.

23 August 1628

Portsmouth, England. The Duke of Buckingham is dead, killed by a single stab wound to the chest. King Charles I adores his chief adviser Buckingham – the rest of Britain hates him. So is he killed by a power-mad rival? No. He is killed by a soldier who's upset because he hasn't been paid.

24 August AD 79

Pompeii, Italy. The citizens are minding their own business this hot summer's evening. Suddenly the nearby volcano, Vesuvius, erupts and smothers the town in choking, stinking, suffocating hot ash. Two thousand die but are preserved better than a fishfinger at the North Pole. In 1748, archaeologists happily dig up the gruesome remains.

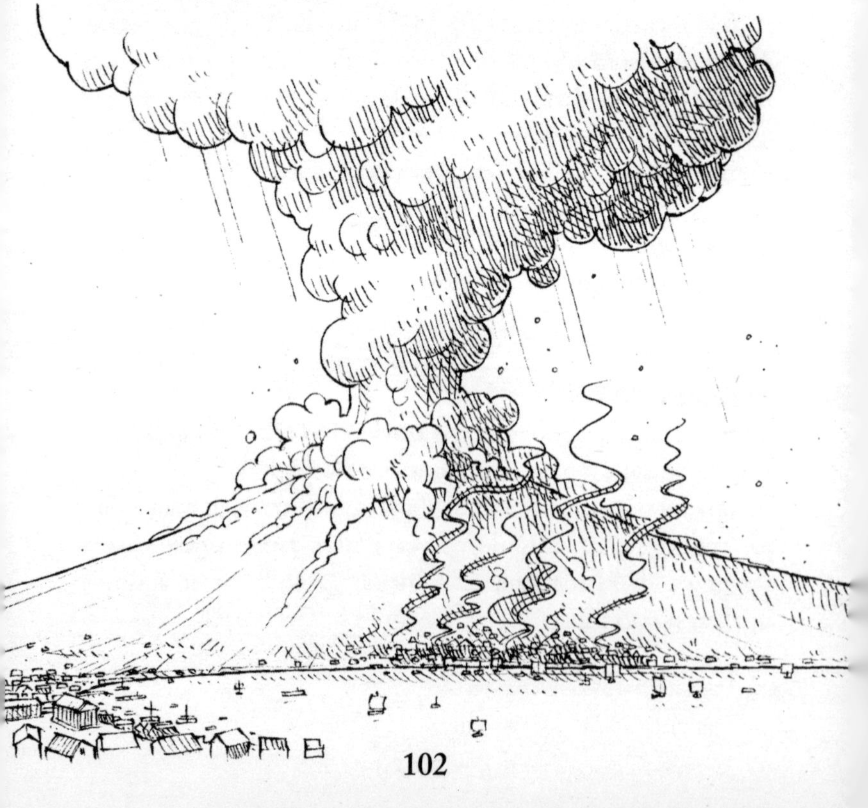

25 August 1530

Ivan the Terrible born in Russia today. By age 13, he is taking part in blood sports like hunting – he has his chief minister hunted down and torn apart by dogs. Later he will kill his own son and have whole cities full of people murdered, including some of his eight wives. (Can't imagine why they call him 'Terrible'.) Eventually he plays one dangerous sport too many. He dies playing … chess.

26 August 1883

Krakatoa Island. The moon turns blue. It's caused by the ash from a huge volcanic eruption as it is scattered through the air. The eruption is heard 3,000 km away and the tidal wave it creates carries a steam ship 3 km into the jungle of a nearby island. Awesome. (This rare event happens just once in a blue moon, you'll be pleased to hear.)

27 August 551 BC
China. Chinese thinker Confucius is born. He is remembered for hundreds of wise proverbs (most of which he probably didn't write) including the brilliant: 'Do not remove a fly from a friend's forehead with a hatchet.' Wow. Over 2,500 years later this is still a sensible bit of advice.

28 August 1719
Durham, England. James Lyon is dead unlucky. He is sentenced to hang today but a pardon is sent to set him free. The messenger goes to the wrong town by mistake. James has a second chance when the gallows break as they try to hang him. They string him up from an oak tree instead. Third time unlucky, Jamie.

29 August 1533
Peru. The Inca chief Atahualpa has been captured by Spanish conqueror, Pizarro. He has paid millions of pounds in ransom to be set free – today Pizarro has him executed anyway.

30 August 30 BC
Egypt. The Greek Queen of Egypt, Cleopatra, is in trouble. The Romans are coming to get her. She probably drinks poison when she hears that her lover Mark Antony has died. Some reports say she stuffs a poisonous snake down her dress and lets it bite her. Were her last words, 'Fangs very much'?

31 August 1422
Vincennes, France. When Henry V dies of dysentery his son takes over. Unfortunately Henry VI is just nine months old. When he opens Parliament at the age of three he cries all the way through the ceremony. Parliaments have been full of whingers ever since.

2 SEPTEMBER 1752 – CALENDAR CORRECTION GETS RID OF 11 DAYS

SEPTEMBER

1 September

Britain. Today is known simply as 'The First' by some people. They mean, 'The first day of the year that hunters are allowed to murder partridges.' So, if you're a partridge, duck. And if you're a duck, duck (in case some shortsighted killer can't tell the difference).

2 September 1752

Britain. Calendars are going to pot because Leap Years aren't quite keeping them in line with the sun. In fact, the shortest day of the year is now 11 days away from when it should be – 21 December. So Britain has to 'lose' 11 days. Simple. After 2 September 1752 the next day will be 14 September 1752. Thousands of people think they are being robbed of 11 days from their lives. There are riots in the streets of many cities. People cry, 'Give us back our 11 days.' (They don't get them.)

3 September 1939

London. It's the Second World War and a 'blackout' of all lights is needed so German bombers can't see the cities. PC George Southworth sees a light in a third-floor window, knocks on the front door but gets no answer. He climbs the drainpipe to reach the room and put the light out himself. He slips – splat. The first of Britain's half-million war deaths.

4 September 1886

Arizona, USA. Apache leader, Geronimo, surrenders. For the last 10 years he's been fighting a guerrilla war against the settlers. He's been trying to persuade them to let the Apaches live in peace. The settlers (and the US Cavalry) have finally won. Final score: Guerrillas 0 – Gorillas 1.

5 September 1715
France. The great king Louis XIV dies today aged 77. He is probably pretty pleased, because doctors damaged his mouth when they tried to take some rotten teeth out. Eating was painful for many years and bits of food often came down his nose. (S'not very nice to have a meal with Big Louis.)

6 September 1776
New York Bay, USA. The British warship, *Eagle*, lies waiting for the American enemy. But when the attack comes from the American *Turtle*, the crew of the *Eagle* never see it. That's because the *Turtle* is a submarine making the first ever underwater attack. It's not successful. Lucky *Eagle*.

7 September 1838
Northumberland, England. 22-year-old Grace Darling and her dad set off in a little lifeboat to rescue the crew of the shipwrecked *Forfarshire*. Grace gets a darling little medal but dies four years later.

8 September 1157
Oxford, England. Richard I is born. He becomes a legend … but which legend? It depends on which history book you read. Richard is a brave and noble Crusader – or is he a cruel soldier who keeps a supply of prisoners handy so he'll always have someone to eat?

9 September 1583
Atlantic Ocean. Sir Humphrey Gilbert dies. Sir who? The man who planted the first English flag in Newfoundland – which is a great name for a new-found land. Imaginative, eh? Old Humph claimed America for Elizabeth I but today, on the way home, his ship *The Squirrel* sinks. Fancy trying to cross the Atlantic on a squirrel.

10 September 1897
London. George Smith is a taxi driver. Today he drives his electric cab to 165 Bond Street. Unfortunately he doesn't stop there. He drives over the pavement and into the front of number 165. He admits to the police that he's been drinking and becomes the first person to be convicted of drunken driving in Britain. Sadly he won't be the last.

11 September 1777
Brandywine Creek, USA. American hero George Washington fights the British – and loses. Nobody's perfect. George was moody, unfriendly and big-headed. He had false teeth made from animal tusks or pulled from enslaved people who probably weren't that keen on losing them to him.

12 September 1609
North America. Henry Hudson in his ship the *Half Moon*, discovers a river unknown to Europeans. He could call it Half Moon River or James River (after his king) but, no. He calls it after himself. Hudson River. Wonder if the Dead Sea was discovered by Mr Dead?

13 September 490 BC
Marathon, Greece. Persia invades Greece with a huge force. The Spartan Greeks can't come to the battle today – they're too busy having a religious ceremony. The little army from the city of Athens faces the might of Persia alone. Amazingly, the Athenians win a famous victory on the battlefield at Marathon. A messenger runs almost 26 miles to take the good news back to Athens then drops dead. People are still doing this (running 26-mile 'marathons', and dropping dead).

14 September
Old England. Nutting Day, when children skip through the fields and go nutting. (The lazy ones stay at home and do nuttin'.) This was an excuse for a day off school in Old England. Maybe you can try it on a teacher today?

15 September 1830
Liverpool, England. The grand opening of the new Liverpool to Manchester railway. All the great men of England are there for the celebration and thousands

line the route. The Duke of Wellington sees his friend William Huskisson and calls him over. Huskisson steps on to the track ... and into the path of the *Rocket* locomotive. Crunch. The *Rocket* isn't damaged but Huskisson's death spoils the party just a bit.

16 September 1420
Spain. Happy birthday to Tomas de Torquemada. But instead of birthday candles, Tom burns people. Tom is a monk with the job of sorting out people who are a danger to the Church in Spain. Tom will burn 2,000 and torture many thousands more by stretching them on the rack. A monk of nasty habits.

17 September 1908
USA. Everyone remembers that Orville and Wilbur Wright were the first men to fly in an aeroplane (17 December 1903). Most people forget Lieutenant Selfridge. On this day Orville takes Selfridge up for a spin to show his wonderful aeroplane to the US Army. A propeller cracks and they crash. Selfridge becomes the first person to die in an air crash. Orville survives but never flies again.

18 September
St Joseph's Day. There is more chance of being kicked to death by a donkey than being killed in an air crash. This could be due to St Joe, the patron saint of air travellers. Joseph of Cupertino was a monk who amazed everyone with his very useful ability to float in the air.

19 September 1356
Poitiers, France. In the Hundred Years War the English face the French at Poitiers. A Scotsman advises the French knights to get off their horses and attack on foot. English knights (on horses) knock them over like skittles and win. Whap. Good knight, sleep tight.

20 September 356 BC
Macedon. Alexander the Great is born. He takes over power in Macedon when his dad is murdered. In fact, ruthless Alex might have had something to do with his dad's death. He goes on to conquer lots of people like Greeks and Persians. At the age of 32 Alexander the Great becomes Alex the Late. Was he poisoned?

21 September 1921
New York, USA. René Fonck sets off today to be the first to fly from New York to Paris. He needs a super-light plane. René's machine has a cabin lined with Spanish leather and (very heavy) mahogany wood, a celebration dinner from the French President is waiting in Paris and lots of prezzies. It races down the runway, the wheels collapse and it disintegrates, killing two passengers. The French President never gets that dinner.

22 September 1515
Holland. Anne of Cleves is born. The Dutch send her picture to Henry VIII and he decides to make her his fourth wife. When he sees her in the flesh he thinks she looks more like a

horse than a woman. He has a bit of a nerve since he wouldn't win any beauty contests himself.

23 September 480 BC
Salamis, Greece. The Greeks meet the Persians in a sea battle. Some Greek captains begin to run away till they meet a ghostly ship which tells them to go back and they will win. They believe the ghost, go back to the battle and send the Persians packing. Amazing ... but true?

24 September 1887
China. The river Huang He breaks free of its banks and sends huge flood waves across the plains. It is probably the world's greatest disaster ever. As many as 2 million die.

25 September 1769
London. Britain sees its first cremation because Honoretta Pratt has left orders that her body should be burned in its grave. She was worried that 'vapours arising from graves may be harmful to the citizens'.

26 September 1854
Balaclava Day. During the Crimean war the British 'Light Brigade' of horse soldiers are ordered to charge at the Russian guns. Out of the roughly 670 men who took part in the charge, around 110 were killed. Many more were wounded or taken prisoner. They are remembered as heroes. The 375 dead horses are forgotten.

27 September 1601
France. Young Prince Louis is born on this day. He will grow up to be Louis XIII. But he celebrates his seventh birthday (today in 1608) by having a bath. That's unusual. It will be the first bath he has ever had in his life.

28 September
Britain. Crack-nut Night. (Not one word of a lie.) Also known as Nut-crack Night. (Honest.) Today is known as Michaelmas Day to celebrate St Michael the Archangel, who is seen as the leader of the armies of heaven that protect us against evil. Some people will roast nuts until they are cracked. (The nuts, not the people.)

29 September
Britain. Pack Rag Day. This is the day when servants and farm workers were hired – or fired. They would wrap their rags in a pack and move to their new home. A good day to change schools – sort of Pack Book Day.

30 September 1913
English Channel. Rudolf Diesel was a great inventor. No prizes for guessing that he invented an engine. But today he is on a cross-channel steamer … and he vanishes. If Diesel ended up in the water surely there'd be an oil slick?

GUNFIGHT AT THE OK CORRAL 1881
STATUE OF LIBERTY 1886

OCTOBER

1 October 1788

Edinburgh, Scotland. William Brodie was a respectable man and a skilled craftsman. He even designed Edinburgh gallows. Yet, today, he is swinging from those gallows. He gambled away his fortune and took to burglary to keep up his rich life. Respectable by day, villainous by night, like the book character, Dr Jekyll and Mr Hyde. In fact that book character was almost certainly based on William Brodie.

2 October 1576

Harwich, England. Explorer Martin Frobisher returns to England a hero, because he comes back with black earth containing, it is said … gold. The London goldsmiths can't find a way to melt the gold – probably because it is a type of iron called 'fool's gold'. Frobisher will return to Canada to prove them wrong. In 1577 he comes back with two hundred tons of 'gold' stuffed into his ship. Elizabeth I locks it in the Tower of London for safety. Two hundred tons of worthless rock. Sorry, Captain Frobisher, but it's fool's gold again. You don't get much more of a fool than that.

3 October 1720

Moscow, Russia. Peter the Great has a very nasty collection of freaks, including five-footed sheep. Today he adds something new when he has his girlfriend executed and keeps her pickled head in a jar in his room. That's love for you.

4 October 1930

France. A giant British airship, the R101, sets off on its

maiden flight. A spiritualist said three days ago that it would crash in flames. And, sure enough, it does. The spiritualist will go on to talk to the captain of the airship – after he is dead, naturally – and he will explain why he crashed.

5 October 1914

France. The first ever air battle. French and German aircraft fly around and shoot pistols at each other. Later the French planes will carry loads of bricks, fly over the German planes and drop the bricks on to them. (Honest.)

6 October 1014

Bulgaria. The Bulgarian army gropes its way back home, defeated by Basil the Byzantine Emperor. Defeated – and de-eyed, because Basil has had the Bulgarians blinded. One man in every hundred has been left with one eye so he can guide his comrades back to their homeland. Bulgarian leader Samuel is so upset by the defeat he has a fit and dies.

7 October 1849

USA. Edgar Allen Poe dies today. A clever writer who wrote cheerful little stories like 'Arthur Gordon Pym of Nantucket'. In this terrible tale three survivors of a shipwreck kill and eat a fourth. Amazingly three survivors of a real-life shipwreck will kill and eat a fourth in the year 1884. A coincidence? Or had they read Poe's book and decided to try his recipe?

8 October 1871
Chicago, USA. Kate O'Leary goes to milk her cow but she's had too much whiskey. (Alice, not the cow.) The cow kicks over a lantern and sets the barn ablaze ... and that sets the rest of Chicago on fire. Eighteen thousand buildings wrecked and 250 people dead.

9 October 1779
Manchester, England. New machines can do the work of several cotton-workers – so the bosses sack the workers. So the workers attack the machines. Later Ned Ludd of Sherwood Forest becomes leader of the wreckers. But in the end the machines will win.

10 October 1903
England. The Women's Social and Political Union is formed by Emmeline Pankhurst. This was one of the more violent groups fighting for the vote for women using methods such as arson, planting bombs in government buildings and politician's homes and even assassination attempts. Unfortunately many saw these techniques as useless, and it took 15 years before women were finally allowed to vote (as long as you met the very strict criteria of being over 30 and either owned a home, were married to a man who owned a home or had graduated from university – simple!).

11 October 1865
Jamaica. Morant Bay Rebellion. Enslaved people in Jamaica were 'free' after 1834 but the owners were still in control.

The Jamaicans had to work for a penny a day. In 1835, an angry mob of 500 ex-slaves marched on the town of Stony Gut armed with sticks, cutlasses, fishing spears and a few guns. The town guard turned out to face them. But who started the trouble? The women. The women had marched into town with their baskets full of stones and they began to throw them. When a stone hit the commander of the guard he ordered his men to open fire. The crowd rushed at them and the soldiers began a murderous massacre.

12 October 1492

West Indies. Captain Christopher Columbus thinks the world is round (while we can all see it's flat). He sails west and bumps into a lump of land that becomes known as the New World. Great news for Europe who will kill the indigenous people and rob their lands – bad news for the people who lose their land and their lives. A truly horrible day in their history.

13 October AD 54

Emperor Claudius dies. He limped, had a cackling laugh, a stammer and a runny nose – sometimes all at the same time. Now he has eaten his last meal. Romans say his wife poisoned him with mushrooms so her son could become emperor. On the other hand modern historians think he simply had a heart attack.

14 October 1066

Hastings, England. Norman William the Conqueror invades and battles against English King Harold. The English hold

Senlac Hill against all the Norman attacks. The Norman soldiers start to run away. The English think they've won and leave the safety of their hilltop. Big mistake. Norman archers can now get at the English leaders. Harold fights on despite an arrow in the eye but dies, hacked to pieces.

It's England's most famous battle but how much do you know about it? Just answer **True** or **False**…

1. William fell in the sea when he landed.

2. Before the battle William put on his chain mail back to front.

3. William wore a rabbit's foot for luck.

4. The Norman attack was led by a juggler.

5. The English were packed so tight that the dead and wounded couldn't fall to the ground.

6. William was known as 'the Conqueror' because he liked playing conkers.

7. King Harold was killed with an arrow in his eye.

8. The Normans knew they'd killed Harold because he wore a crown.

9. The Normans said they buried Harold under a rose bush.

10. The English said Harold DIDN'T die at Hastings.

Answers

1. True. He stumbled and fell forward as he reached the beach. Ooops! His men gasped. A bad sign. But witty Will grabbed some pebbles, stood up and said, 'See how I have grabbed England?'

2. True. It was another unlucky sign. William just laughed and said, 'This is the day I "turn" from Duke to King.'

3. False. William wore the bones of Saint Rasyphus and Saint Ravennus around his neck for luck.

4. True. The Normans didn't want to attack up hill and risk their lives. At 9 am the minstrel Taillefer began to juggle with his sword and sing a battle song. He attacked – an English warrior moved forward to meet him and Taillefer lopped off his head. Taillefer moved on – the English shields parted to let him through where they hacked him down. He died.

5. True.

6. False.

7. False. Harold was WOUNDED with an arrow to the eye. But he was KILLED when Norman knights charged forward and hacked him to bits.

8. False. Harold's face was smashed. Only his wife knew his corpse because she could spot its unique marks.

9. False. They said King Harold's corpse was taken to the sea shore and buried under a pile of stones. The English gave him a headstone reading, 'Harold, you rest here, to guard the sea and shore.'

10. True. The English told a story that Harold survived, buried under a pile of bodies. A peasant woman found him and nursed him back to health. He hid in a cellar in Winchester for two years before leading attacks on the hated Normans. In time he got religion and became Harold the hermit.

15 October 1529

Vienna, Austria. The Ottoman (Turkish) army of Suleiman has been sweeping through Europe. It seems unstoppable … until today. It reaches Vienna but fails to capture the city. But what really defeats Suleiman and his men are hunger and disease. On this day he retreats, which is just as well – if he'd won then you might have been reading this in Turkish.

16 October 1408

Pont-de-l'Arche, France. A public executioner sends in his bill for keeping a prisoner in jail and executing him. There is an extra charge for a length of rope for tying up this prisoner. Why didn't the prisoner untie it and escape? Because the prisoner was a pig. Tried, found guilty and hanged for killing a child. Oink.

17 October 1605

Agra, India. Emperor Akbar dies. But, was he poisoned?

Who knows? Who cares? So many people want him dead that the list of suspects reads like the Kolkata phone book. He attacked enemy fortresses and massacred everyone inside. Other historians say he was a wise ruler who brought peace.

18 October 1216
England. King John dies on this day after eating too many peaches and drinking too much cider. He was trying to cheer himself up after losing the crown jewels in an accident. He could be cruel and had the odd person bumped off – his own nephew, Arthur, and his wife's new boyfriend. It's said he won't rest easy in his grave because he's a vampire. (A batty idea.)

19 October
St Isaac Jogues' Day. Isaac is a United States martyr in the United States but a Canadian martyr in Canada. He goes to make peace with the native Iroquois people in 1646 … but the Mohawks get him first. This is no joke … and soon, it's no Jogue either.

20 October 1714
London. King George I is crowned today. His German 'Hanover' family have taken over from the slimy Stuarts … but Stuart supporters will try to rebel. When they do, their leaders are executed. Cruel George is unpopular – especially when he goes off to dance at a ball while the noble rebels are being beheaded.

21 October 1805
The British fleet have defeated the French at Trafalgar. They were led by Lord Nelson, but old Nelson has been shot. To get his body safely back to England for burial the sailors pickle it in a barrel of brandy. It's not wasted though. They will later drink the brandy. Yeuch.

22 October 1797
Paris, France. Andre-Jacques Garnerin jumps out of a hot-air balloon to test his new invention – the parachute. He doesn't know that it should have a hole in the top to let the air flow smoothly through. As a result he has a bumpy ride. He lands safely, but his breakfast lands first – on watchers below.

23 October 1642
Edgehill, England. The first battle in the English Civil War between the armies of King Charles I and Parliament. Famous surgeon William Harvey is there after the battle, in which many men die. Harvey is so used to dead bodies that when he grows cold he simply pulls a corpse over him for warmth.

24 October 1901
Niagara Falls, USA. Mrs Ann Edson Taylor was desperate for cash to pay the mortgage on her house, so she came up with an incredible stunt – she sailed over Niagara Falls in a barrel. And she lived. Warning: do not try this in your local river.

25 October 1415
Agincourt, France. The French army of 14–20,000 men are beaten by Henry V's English army of 6–8,000 men. The English lost 600 but the French had 6,000 killed. Then the English cut the throats of 1,000 French prisoners. Very unsporting, Henry.

26 October 1881
Tombstone, USA. Marshall Wyatt Earp and his brothers come face to face with the Clanton and McLaury families. In the famous 'Gunfight at the OK Corral', Wyatt wins. Three Clanton and McLaury gunmen die while two run away and live.

27 October 1901
Paris, France. Three men go into a shop and rob it. Nothing unusual about that? But they run out and jump into a motor car. They go down in history as the first criminals to use a getaway car. British police are so worried by this new type of crime they set up the Flying Squad with fast cars ... 18 years later.

28 October 1886
New York, USA. The French people have given the American people a prezzie: a dirty great 46-metre woman with a flaming torch called the Statue of Liberty. It was a gift but the mean US government now refuse to pay the $100,000 needed for the statue's base. The money is raised by the *New York World* newspaper. What a liberty.

29 October 1740
Scotland. James Boswell is born today. He becomes famous for writing about the Englishman Doctor Johnson. But Doctor Johnson said some pretty nasty things about Boswell's Scotland. Johnson said the best thing to come out of Scotland was the road to England. Cruel.

30 October 1938
USA. Actor Orson Welles broadcasts his production of *The War of the Worlds* on the radio. He makes it sound like a news broadcast ... and thousands of people believe they are

listening to reports of a Martian invasion. They panic. Later broadcasts tell them it's only a play – but the panickers refuse to believe it.

31 October
Hallowe'en is short for All Hallow's Eve, or the day before All Saints' Day. It was probably first celebrated by the Druids of ancient Britain, who believed that on this evening, Saman (the lord of the dead) calls up evil spirits. The Druids would light great fires on Hallowe'en, to keep the spirits away. (If an evil spirit lives in Hell then it won't be worried by a little bonfire, will it?) For the Celts, Hallowe'en was their New Year's Eve and a good time for fortune telling. They also believed that the ghosts revisited their old homes tonight.

REMEMBRANCE DAY – 11 NOVEMBER

NOVEMBER

1 November

Britain. First day of the fox-hunting season. Oscar Wilde called fox-hunting 'the unspeakable in pursuit of the uneatable'. About 30,000 foxes died each year. A hunting ban means fewer foxes are killed by packs of hounds. But they can still be a nuisance so farmers shoot them instead. It's no fun being a fox.

2 November

Mexico. The Day of the Dead. The Mexicans don't forget you just because you are dead – well, not every day. On this day they have celebrations in graveyards when they offer flowers, food, toys, gifts and lighted candles to the dead.

3 November 1926

Annie Oakley dies. She was famous as a sharpshooter with Buffalo Bill's Wild West Show. She wasn't actually from the Wild West, but she was a very good shot. People used to flock to see Annie shoot while standing on the bare back of a horse and riding a speeding bicycle.

4 November

Northern England. Mischief Night. A time when children are expected to get up to jolly little jokes and pranks. Unfortunately, these days, they prefer to sit with their square eyes gazing at a screen. In the good old days, they'd be persecuting pensioners, torturing tomcats and tormenting teachers.

5 November 1605

On this day Guy Fawkes is caught before he blows up Parliament. He was arrested before midnight on the fifth so really we should be crying, 'Remember, remember the fourth of November'. In Britain people celebrate with fireworks, which will kill far more people over the next 400 years than Guy ever did.

6 November 1860

USA. Abraham Lincoln elected President. Not popular with some people. Like the man who wrote to him, 'God damn your God damned old hell-fired God damned soul to Hell God damn you and goddam your God damned family's God damned soul to Hell.' Perhaps he voted for the other fella?

7 November 1846

Massachusetts, USA. 21-year-old Alice Mohan is the first person to have a limb cut off using anaesthetic. The doctors took off her right leg after sending her to sleep with ether.

8 November 1519
Mexico. The Aztec natives of Mexico have an old prophecy that a fair-skinned god will appear among them. Today he arrives. Little do they know that this 'god' is actually Spanish conqueror Hernán Cortés. He kidnaps their king, Moctezuma, and pinches their gold. When the Aztecs discover the truth about Cortés they stone King Moctezuma to death.

9 November 1888
London, England. The police have the Whitechapel area surrounded, trying to stop one man ... but he still gets through. He kills Mary Jane Kelly, his fifth and final victim tonight. He will never be caught, and he will never kill again, but his nickname will become a legend – 'Jack the Ripper'.

10 November 1945
New York, USA. The last member of the famous Bonaparte family, Jerome Napoleon Bonaparte, died in 1945. He was fatally injured when he tripped over his dog's lead in Central Park, New York, and broke his neck.

11 November
Remembrance Day. The last day of the horrific First World War ... and now all war dead are remembered on this day. The red poppy is a symbol of the day, after a Canadian poet wrote about the graveyards, 'In Flanders fields the poppies blow, between the crosses, row on row.' Thousands of poppies – sadly 16.5 million war casualties outnumber them.

12 November 1035
England. King Canute (or Cnut) the Great dies. Famous for sitting on the beach and telling the tide to go back. It didn't and Cnut turned to his followers and said, 'See. I'm not as powerful as you creeps try to make out. Let that be a lesson to you … and pass me a dry pair of socks.'

13 November 1687
London. King Charles II's favourite girlfriend dies. Her name is Nell Gwyn and she's just 37 years old. She has had two boyfriends called Charles before the King – so she calls Charles the Second her Charles the Third.

14 November 1896
Britain. The speed limit for cars is raised from 4 mph to 14 mph. Those fellas with red flags who used to walk in front of the cars will be a) sacked b) run over, or c) Olympic champ sprinters.

15 November 1872
New York, USA. The ship *Dei Gratia* leaves harbour and sails towards one of the world's greatest mysteries. Three weeks later the crew come across a drifting ship without a soul on board. Where did they go? Were they murdered, abducted by aliens, or did they just jump overboard? No one knows what happened to the crew of that famous ship … the *Mary Celeste*.

16 November 1724

London. Jack Sheppard's luck finally runs out at the end of a hangman's rope. The expert locksmith and thief escaped four times from jails he was held in. Two groups of friends try to revive him after he's been hanged – but in fighting over the body they kill him off.

17 November 1745

England. The Profound Oaths Act makes swearing a criminal offence. Say 'Gog's Malt' and you risk a fine and a whipping. Not a lot of people take any notice of this law but it stays a law until 1967.

18 November

St Mawes' Day. Some saints died hard. Mawes is born hard on this day when his mother is thrown into the sea in a barrel. Mawes is born in the barrel and five months later the mother and baby are washed ashore in Ireland. When Mawes finally dies, his miracles aren't over. Earth from his grave, mixed with water, is a miracle medicine. (But it tastes dead awful.)

19 November 1566

Herefordshire, England. Robert Devereux is born. He grows up to be the Earl of Essex and a special favourite of Elizabeth I – in fact she really fancies him ... until he tries to lead a rebellion against her. The brave Earl once saved the life of a man called Derrick. And it is Derrick who has the pleasure of beheading the Earl in 1601. There's gratitude for you.

20 November AD 870
England. King Edmund fights the Viking invaders. Bad move. They tie him to a tree and fire arrows at him till he has more holes than a pepper-pot lid. Then they pull out his lungs and cut off his head. Edmund accidentally dies as a result of this treatment.

21 November 1864
Sand Creek, USA. A Cheyenne camp is attacked by soldiers led by Colonel John Chivington. Among the 230 Cheyenne dead are 105 women and children. The local newspaper declares, 'Colorado soldiers have again covered themselves with glory.' Cheyenne scalps are strung across the stage of the local theatre while people roar, 'Exterminate them.' Sadly the audience are not talking about the soldiers.

22 November 1922
Egypt. Howard Carter and Lord Carnarvon open the tomb of Tutankhamun for the first time in 3,000 years. In just a few months, Carnarvon is dead. Is it a mummy's curse? It could be – for not only is Carnarvon dead ... when Carter opens the coffin he finds Tutankhamun is dead too.

23 November 1718
The North American coast. The infamous pirate Blackbeard is shot, his head cut off and stuck on the front of the ship. His body is thrown over the side, then it is said to have swam round the ship three times.

24 November 1963
Dallas, USA. Lee Harvey Oswald shot and killed President John F Kennedy two days ago. Tonight a man shoots Oswald dead. But did Oswald really do it at all? Some people say he was innocent. Oswald says nothing.

25 November
St Catherine's Day. Around the fourth century young Cath was tortured by being tied to a wheel and having her bones broken. The wheel collapsed. A miracle. Catherine's wheel has a firework named after it. Sadly, the sword used to behead her didn't collapse.

26 November 1703
England. The country is hit by severe gales known as the Great Storm. It wrecks lighthouses ... and heavy houses too. 8,000 people die and thousands of trees die too. That's not what they are there fir.

27 November 1914
Grantham, England. It's the First World War and men have gone off to fight leaving women to do their jobs. Today

sees the first policewomen employed, Ms Allen and Ms Harburn. Ms Allen knows lots about the law, having spent two terms in jail while fighting for votes for women. Men (and policemen) have made sexist jokes ever since – 'I say. It's a fair cop. Ho. Ho.' (Yawn, yawn.)

28 November 1757
England. Poet William Blake is born today. This Blake bloke is seriously weird. He claims to have chatted to people from history including prophets from the Bible. His wife becomes fed up because she hardly ever sees him. Maybe Blake is in Heaven instead of home?

29 November
St Andrew's Eve. Not a lot of people know this – and don't spread it around … BUT on this night all buried treasure sends up a faint glow through the ground. Take a spade and wander the ancient sites tonight. By morning you'll be rich … if you don't die first of cold/fright/angry-farmer's shotgun.

30 November
St Andrew is Scotland's own saint. Old Andy was a disciple of Jesus and was crucified on an X-shaped cross. That's why Scotland's flag is a white X-shaped cross. Of course, it could have been a ✛-shaped cross that fell on its side.

PERILS OF POWER

DECEMBER

1 December 1955

Rosa Parks was on a bus in Alabama, USA. She refused to give up her seat to a white passenger. The Alabama laws at that time said Black passengers had to sit in the back and to give up their seats to white passengers if the white section was full. The bus driver ordered Parks and three other Black passengers to move. The other three obeyed, but Rosa Parks refused to stand up and give her seat. She became a hero of Black Americans.

2 December 1859

West Virginia, USA. John Brown's body lies mouldering in the grave today. That's because he's been executed. His crime? He led a rebellion to free enslaved Americans. They raided an ammunition store at Harper's Ferry to get guns for his rebels. They killed seven people there and Brown was charged with murder.

3 December 1926

England. Famous mystery writer Agatha Christie is involved in her very own mystery when she disappears for 10 days. Where is she? Is she alive? Has she lost her memory? Who cares? Actually 15,000 people care – that's how many join the search and find her in Harrogate. No one ever knows how she spent those ten days. It's a Christie mystery.

4 December

St Barbara's Day. Turkish girl Barbie was locked in a tower by her father. Her very protective father. But she becomes a

Christian and daddy becomes a bit upset. He cuts her head off. (That's more than a bit upset to be honest.) But a really upset God blasts daddy with lightning. ('Why couldn't he do this before Barbie died?' you might well ask.) Barbara is now the patron saint of lightning and guns.

5 December 1484

Rome, Italy. Pope Innocent VIII changes the rules about witchcraft. It had been a small offence before today but now it becomes a serious crime. He orders the Holy Inquisition to seek out and destroy witches. In the next 300 years about 200,000 people will die cruel deaths, accused of being witches. Most of these are women, often old and defenceless.

6 December 1957

USA. The 'space-race' is on between Russia and the USA. Two months ago Russia launched the first satellite called *Sputnik*. Russia 1, USA 0. Today the US launches *Atlas* with its first satellite. It rises less than a metre off the ground then explodes. Russia 2, USA 0. Russia experimented with mice, insects and dogs in rockets. At first they all died.

7 December 1733

Newcastle-upon-Tyne, England. A report on this day says, 'A flying man flew down from the top of the castle keep. After that he made an ass fly down, by which several accidents happened. The weights tied to the ass's legs knocked down several people, bruised others in a dreadful manner and killed a girl upon the spot.' They probably used a sort of parachute. (It would be nice to think the ass survived.)

8 December 1626
Sweden. Queen Christina is born and grows up to be a little odd. She is terrified of fleas and has a miniature cannon built to defend herself. The barrel measures 10 cm and it works like a real cannon, firing miniature cannon balls.

9 December 1783
London. A new sports stadium opens. The stadium is Newgate Prison and the sport is hanging criminals in public. The trouble is that more people are murdered in the crowd than on the scaffold as cut-throats throttle and rob the watchers. After 1868, criminals are hanged inside the prison walls in private.

10 December 1603
Winchester, England. Walter Raleigh, who is often accused of introducing tobacco to Britain, lays his head on the block. He's about to be executed for treason. At the last second, King James sends a reprieve. Raleigh goes to the block again, for the same crime, 15 years later ... but this time the axe falls.

11 December 1282

Builth Wells, Wales. Prince Llywelyn, killed in battle with the English today, is the last real Welsh Prince of Wales. Llywelyn should have been captured but squire Stephen de Frankton doesn't recognise the prince and kills him by mistake. The Prince of Wales's head will decorate the Tower of London walls. Last Prince of Wales, first Prince of Walls?

12 December 1955

New York, USA. A landmark in the history of popular music. Singer Bill Haley records a song which goes, 'See you later alligator, in a while crocodile'. Many pop songs have been banned for their words. Sadly this one wasn't.

13 December 1862

Fredericksburg, USA. General Jackson has a great idea. His men will swim naked across the Rappahannock river and attack the enemy on a snowy December night. They won't wear uniforms because they would soak up the water and weigh the men down, he thinks. Luckily the plan is abandoned.

14 December 1650

Oxford, England. Anne Greene is hanged for murdering her child. Doctors take her body away to practise on ... but she starts breathing. Within five days she is fit and well. Her friends say it's a miracle and proves she is innocent after all. She is pardoned and lives to get married and have three more children.

15 December AD 37
Rome, Italy. Emperor Nero is born. As emperor he sees a collapsible boat used in a stage play and orders one for his mother. He then arranges for it to collapse while she is at sea. She swims ashore so Nero simply has her assassinated by men with big swords. That works better.

16 December 1797
Prussia. King Frederick William II is dying. Lots of people rush to bring him miracle cures in the hope that they'll make a quick bag of gold. Fred Will is told to breathe in the breath of two new born calves, to sleep between two nine-year-old children and to listen to wind instruments ... but violins will kill him. (You've heard school orchestras, so you'll understand this.) Fred Will tries them all and dies anyway.

17 December 1903
North Carolina, USA. Aviation brothers Orville and Wilbur Wright made the first powered flight with their invention, the Wright Flyer. It only managed a maximum of 260 m (852 ft), and Orville, later said, 'No flying machine will ever fly from New York to Paris.' Which just goes to prove, 'Two Wrights do make a wrong.'

18 December 1912
Sussex, England. At last old bones are found which show the missing link between monkeys and human beings. The skull of the 'Piltdown Man' is found. Scientists are really excited

for the next 40 years – till it is proved to be a big fake and a huge joke. Someone made a monkey of the scientists.

19 December 1547
England. A new law says tramps should be branded with a 'V' (for Vagrant) if they don't go back to their home town. First warning gets a whipping. Later they can be enslaved for two years. This new law is good news for tramps: the last law in 1535 said they could be executed.

20 December 1590
France. Doctor Ambroise Paré dies. He was an expert at treating battle wounds. He used the neat trick of tying off leaking blood vessels. Before Paré, doctors used to seal open wounds by dipping them in boiling oil. Sizzle.

21 December
Britain. Mumping Day. The day when poor people go 'mumping' ... knocking on the doors of the rich and begging for food, money or clothes. They could get threatening – maybe they said, 'I'm a mumper, gizza jumper or I'll thump yer.'

22 December AD 640
Alexandria. A sad day for book lovers. The library at Alexandria is supposed to contain all the books of the world. When the Muslim armies capture Alexandria they decide that the parchment scrolls will make really useful fuel to heat

the waters of the public baths of the city ... well, it is winter after all. Six months later they're all burned.

23 December 1888
Holland. Famous painter Vincent van Gogh gets really upset when he has an argument with another painter, Gauguin. Vince cuts his own ear off. When someone asks, 'Why did you do that?' van Gogh replies, 'Eh?' This brilliant painter had a sad end when he shot himself in the chest. He was just 37 years old.

24 December 1914
Dover, England. A vicar sees a light in the sky. There is a strange noise, then a brilliant flash. The Christmas star? No, a German airship dropping the first ever bomb on British soil. It falls in the vicar's garden and makes sure his Christmas goes with a bang.

25 December AD 390
Roman Empire. Roman Emperor, Theodosius, is saying 'Sorry.' to the people of Thessalonica – or at least to the ones who are left alive. The people had a little riot and Theodosius decided to teach them a lesson. He had the rioters massacred.

Still, it's nice of old Theo to say, 'Sorry … and have a very happy Christmas.'

26 December
Boxing Day is so called because rich people used to give their servants Christmas 'boxes' today. Yesterday the servants were far too busy stuffing and cooking the rich people's turkeys. Poor servants get their Christmas a day late … but it still beats the heck out of that turkey's Christmas.

27 December 1539
Rochester, England. Henry VIII has a favourite minister, Thomas Cromwell. Cromwell has persuaded Henry to marry Anne of Cleves, who arrives in England on this day. Henry hates Anne but he doesn't have her head cut off. Instead he divorces her … and has Thomas Cromwell's head cut off.

28 December
Innocents' Day. An unlucky day. Back on the first Christmas Day when Jesus was born, King Herod ordered the slaughter of all the male children in Bethlehem to make sure this new king (Jesus) didn't grow up to nick his throne. The Three Wise Men had said that would happen. Hundreds of 'innocent' children die. Three Wise Men were unwise to open their three wise mouths.

29 December 1170
Canterbury, England. Archbishop of Canterbury, Thomas

Becket, is in bits after an argument with King Henry II's knights. Henry was really rather cut up by the killing – but not so cut up as Becket. They cut him down near the altar in the church and he dies when his brains spill out.

30 December 1916

Russia. Rasputin 'The Mad Monk' is a favourite of the Russian Tsar and he practically runs the country. A group of jealous lords invite Rasputin to a midnight tea party. Rasputin tucks into food sprinkled with cyanide ... but doesn't die. They shoot him twice ... but he doesn't die. They shoot him four more times as he escapes, beat him with chains and throw him into the icy Neva River. He dies. Some tea party.

31 December AD 192

Rome, Italy. Emperor Commodus decides to celebrate the new year with a sacrifice of his consuls (government ministers). The consuls don't want to be sacrificed for some reason. Commodus's girlfriend hires an athlete called Narcissus to strangle Commodus in his bath. Happy New Year to new Emperor Pertinax, who lasts three whole months before he is assassinated too. Isn't history horrible?

TERRY DEARY

Terry Deary was born at a very early age, so long ago he can't remember. But his mother, who was there at the time, says he was born in Sunderland, northeast England, in 1946 – so it's not true that he writes all Horrible Histories from memory. At school he was a horrible child only interested in playing football and giving teachers a hard time. His history lessons were so boring and so badly taught, that he learned to loathe the subject. Horrible Histories is his revenge.

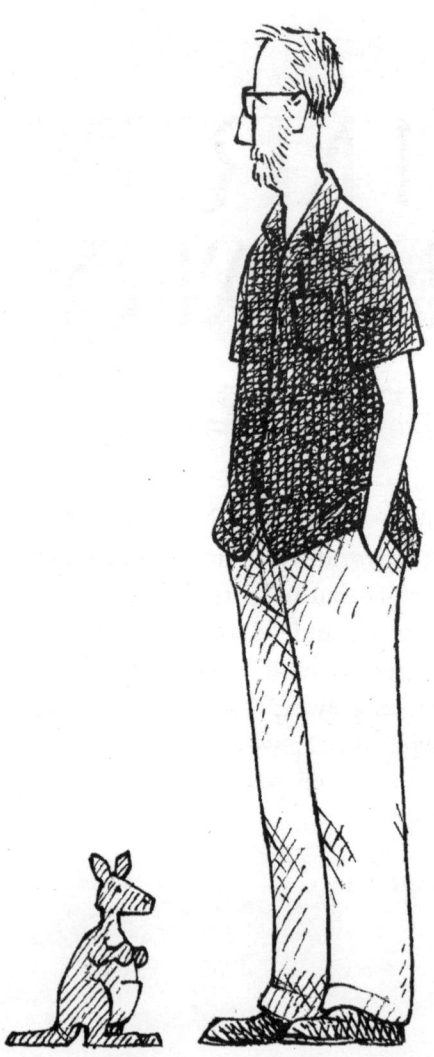

MARTIN BROWN

Martin Brown was born in Melbourne, on the proper side of the world. Ever since he can remember he's been drawing. His dad used to bring back huge sheets of paper from work and Martin would fill them with doodles and little figures. Then, quite suddenly, with food and water, he grew up, moved to the UK and found work doing what he's always wanted to do: drawing doodles and little figures.

A YEAR. 365 DAYS.
WHAT'S THE WORST THAT
COULD HAPPEN?

QUITE A LOT,
AS IT GOES.